ORYX AND CRAKE

Margaret Atwood

*spark notes

SPARKNOTES is a registered trademark of SparkNotes LLC

© 2020 SparkNotes LLC
This 2020 edition printed for SparkNotes LLC by Sterling Publishing Co., Inc.

ISBN 978-1-4114-8044-5

Distributed in Canada by Sterling Publishing Co., Inc.
c/o Canadian Manda Group, 664 Annette Street
Toronto, Ontario, M6S 2C8, Canada
Distributed in the United Kingdom by GMC Distribution Services
Castle Place, 166 High Street, Lewes, East Sussex, BN7 1XU, England
Distributed in Australia by NewSouth Books
University of New South Wales, Sydney, NSW 2052, Australia

For information about custom editions, special sales, and premium
and corporate purchases, please contact Sterling Special Sales at
800-805-5489 or specialsales@sterlingpublishing.com.

Manufactured in Canada

Lot #:
2 4 6 8 10 9 7 5 3 1
09/20

sterlingpublishing.com
sparknotes.com

Please email content@sparknotes.com to report any errors.

CONTENTS

CONTEXT

Margaret Atwood is one of Canada's most decorated and famous writers. Over the course of her long and prolific career, she has published more than fifty books of fiction, poetry, and critical essays. However, Atwood remains best known for her novels. Two of those novels have received one of fiction's most prestigious honors: the Booker Prize. Atwood first won the Booker in 2000 for her novel *The Blind Assassin*, and she won again in 2019 for *The Testaments*. In addition to receiving many prestigious honors and awards, Atwood has a large readership. Her fiction became even more popular following the release of the TV show *The Handmaid's Tale*, based on Atwood's 1985 novel of the same name. This series, which began airing in 2017, has won popular and critical acclaim alike, and it has drawn a new generation of readers to Atwood's work.

Margaret Atwood was born in 1939 in Ottawa, Ontario, Canada, and she spent much of her childhood in the heavily forested areas of northern Quebec, where her father conducted research on forest insect life. An insatiable reader from childhood, Atwood felt inclined to a writing career from an early age. She pursued literary studies at university, first at Victoria College at the University of Toronto, where she received a bachelor's degree in 1961, and then at Radcliffe College at Harvard University, where she completed a master's degree in 1962. Although Atwood began work on a doctoral degree, her dissertation, which she never finished, took a backseat to her burgeoning career as a writer. In 1961, she published her first book of poetry, *Double Persephone*. She went on to publish nine more collections of poetry throughout the 1960s and 70s. Her first novel, *The Edible Woman*, was published in 1969. Atwood wrote four more novels before her landmark book *The Handmaid's Tale* appeared in 1985. *The Handmaid's Tale* was a finalist for the Booker Prize, and it won two other important awards: the Governor General's Award for Canadian literature and the Arthur C. Clarke Award for science fiction.

The publication of *The Handmaid's Tale* marked Atwood's growing interest in speculative fiction, a broad category of imaginative fiction that speculates on what could become of the world given the current social, political, and/or technological state of affairs. Although some critics believe that science fiction and fantasy belong under the umbrella of speculative fiction, Atwood distances herself from these genres. As she has stated in numerous public interviews, she understands science fiction as a genre that imagines a world filled with futuristic technologies that do not yet exist. By contrast, speculative fiction imagines events that could really happen given the political and technological means that are already part of our world. In the case of *The Handmaid's Tale*, for example, Atwood explored the possibility of a near-future dystopia in which a totalitarian state replaces the United States government and institutes a repressive patriarchal regime that strips women of all their rights. The dystopian world Atwood imagines in *The Handmaid's Tale* could conceivably happen, and this plausibility gives the novel both its power and relevance for contemporary readers.

Atwood's interest in speculative fiction resurfaced again in 2003 with the publication of *Oryx and Crake*, which was also a finalist for the Booker Prize. As with *The Handmaid's Tale*, Atwood set *Oryx and Crake* in a near-future dystopia that resembles our own in many disturbing ways. *Oryx and Crake* takes place sometime near the end of the twenty-first century, in the aftermath of a catastrophic pandemic that has killed off most of the world's population, leaving only a handful of scattered survivors. The novel moves back and forth between the postapocalyptic present and the pre-apocalyptic past in order to explain how the global catastrophe came about. In the process, *Oryx and Crake* reveals a disturbing logic that could very well lead from our present day to a future disaster. Just as she did in *The Handmaid's Tale*, Atwood uses speculative fiction to direct her readers to important contemporary issues, such as the moral implications of genetic research and the dangers of corporate tyranny. The story of *Oryx and Crake* continues in the other two volumes of Atwood's MaddAddam Trilogy: *The Year of the Flood* and *MaddAddam*, published in 2009 and 2013 respectively.

PLOT OVERVIEW

ryx and Crake opens with a man named Snowman waking up in a tree. Some kind of catastrophic event has taken place, but the reader does not yet know what the event was or what caused the event. It appears that Snowman may be the sole survivor of the event, aside from a group of childlike people he refers to as the "Children of Crake," who walk around naked and clearly have a unique genetic composition.

The postapocalyptic world represents the novel's present time, and each chapter of the book moves back and forth between Snowman's present experiences and his memories of his pre-apocalypse life, when he went by the name Jimmy. These separate but connected narrative threads weave together as the book moves along.

In the present-time narrative, Snowman watches over the Children of Crake, or the "Crakers," to whom he feels a sense of responsibility. Snowman spins fictional stories about individuals named Crake and Oryx, whom the Crakers understand as kinds of gods: whereas Crake watches over the Crakers, Oryx presides over the lives and well-being of plants and animals.

Though the Crakers appear well adapted to the postapocalyptic environment, Snowman struggles to keep himself fed and hydrated. He knows where he can find more much-needed supplies, but the location is far away, and he's never left the Crakers for more than a day. Nevertheless, he decides to make the dangerous journey. After informing the Crakers, he sets off for the Paradice facility in the RejoovenEsense Compound, where he once worked alongside Crake.

On his journey to Paradice, Snowman encounters several threats, including a herd of cunning and dangerous genetically engineered animals called pigoons. Though Snowman is slowed down by an infected foot wound, he eventually reaches Paradice, where he gathers crucial supplies. With his booty in tow, he limps back to the Crakers.

Although Snowman's narrative functions as a frame for the novel, the majority of the book focuses on Snowman's memories of his prior self, Jimmy. This narrative begins with Jimmy's boyhood. His parents worked at a company called OrganInc Farms, which researched ways to grow human organs cheaply and effectively. Jimmy's mother grew increasingly disgusted by the company's work, which caused friction with her husband. She suffered a long period of depression, and soon after her husband got a high-status new job, she ran away, abandoning Jimmy.

Jimmy suffered greatly after his mother's disappearance. However, he survived through a blossoming friendship with a new student at HelthWyzer High named Crake, with whom he spent a lot of time watching graphic videos of sex and violence on the internet. Whereas Jimmy lacked an aptitude for math and science, Crake proved himself gifted in both disciplines. After they graduated, Crake went off to the prestigious Watson-Crick Institute, where he majored in bio-engineering. He graduated early and soon began to lead his own research projects.

Meanwhile, Jimmy attended a lower-tier school specializing in the arts and humanities. There he majored in a program called Problematics, which prepared him for a career in advertising. After graduating, Jimmy started working for a company called AnooYoo, where he applied his dissertation research on twentieth-century self-help manuals to marketing campaigns for self-improvement products. Although Crake and Jimmy kept up with and occasionally visited each other, their communications dwindled as the years progressed.

Occasionally during his years at AnooYoo, employees of an agency called the CorpSeCorps came to Jimmy's apartment to interrogate him about his mother's whereabouts, but Jimmy had long since lost contact with her. In his fifth year at AnooYoo, the agents came again and showed Jimmy a video of his mother's execution. The news of his mother's death sent Jimmy into a profound depression, which only came to an end when Crake showed up at his apartment and asked Jimmy to come work with him at RejoovenEsense. Jimmy accepted the job, which involved running an ad campaign for a new pill called BlyssPluss that Crake had designed to improve users' libido while simultaneously (and secretly) making them unable to have children. Crake presided over an additional top-secret project located in a special facility called Paradice, which housed a new breed of genetically engineered humans: the Crakers.

At Paradice, Jimmy met a woman named Oryx, whom Crake had hired to teach the Crakers and to help distribute the BlyssPluss pills worldwide. Jimmy recognized Oryx from a child pornography video that he and Crake had seen when they were teenagers. Crake had met Oryx in person when he was in college and employed her for sex work. Oryx and Crake developed a relationship, and when Crake started at RejoovenEsense, he hired Oryx to work there too. Oryx seduced Jimmy, and Jimmy worried that Crake would feel jealous if he found out. One night, when Crake was away from the facility and Oryx was picking up takeout, news reports started coming in about simultaneous plague outbreaks unfolding around the world. Oryx called Jimmy to explain that the BlyssPluss pills contained a delayed-release contagion, and that she had unwittingly participated in the outbreak. Crake's plague spread quickly and killed the majority of people on the planet.

In the first hours of the outbreak, Crake returned to Paradice with Oryx in tow, and he slit her throat in front of Jimmy. Jimmy then shot Crake. For the first few weeks after the outbreak, Jimmy remained locked in the Paradice facility alone, searching for reasons that Crake would kill Oryx. Eventually, he introduced himself to the Crakers as "Snowman" and led them to a new home near the ocean, where they still live in the novel's present time.

The novel ends with Snowman's present-time journey from Paradice back to the Crakers. When he arrives, the Crakers inform him that they saw a group of people like him in the area. Snowman tracks down the other humans and wonders whether to approach them as friends or foes.

CHARACTER LIST

Snowman   The protagonist of the novel. Snowman is the survivor of a pandemic, who has been left in charge of a tribe of childlike, genetically enhanced humans that were created by his friend-turned-rival, Crake. Snowman feels lonely and morose as he struggles to survive in postapocalyptic conditions, and he spends much of his time immersed in memories of his pre-apocalypse life, when his name was Jimmy.

Crake   Snowman's longtime friend and rival, and architect of the pandemic. Crake, whose original name was Glenn, showed early promise in math and science and grew into a genius geneticist. Crake's view of the world was coldly rational and fiercely atheistic, and he pursued ambitious but morally questionable genetic research that eventually led to billions of deaths and the genesis of a new breed of enhanced humans.

Oryx   The mutual love interest of Snowman and Crake. Originally from a rural village somewhere in south or southeast Asia, Oryx was sold into slavery at a young age and spent much of her early life working in the sex industry. Despite the numerous traumas of her youth, Oryx retained an optimistic attitude, which made her an excellent teacher for Crake's genetically modified humans.

Sharon   Snowman's mother and a former microbiologist. After growing disenchanted with the work she was doing for OrganInc Farms, Sharon ran away from her job and family. Although Snowman only has glimpses of her life after she abandoned him, he knows she joined the activist group God's Gardeners and participated in demonstrations against research involving genetic manipulation.

Snowman's Father   Unnamed. A genetic researcher at OrganInc
Farms and, later, at HelthWyzer, Snowman's father
was an emotionally distant figure who frequently
expressed cold disappointment about his son's lack
of intellectual ability in math and science. He fought
frequently with his wife Sharon about the moral
implications of his research, arguing that the research
had practical benefits. After his wife ran away, he took
up a relationship with his colleague Ramona.

Ramona   A colleague of Snowman's father. Ramona worked
with Snowman's father at OrganInc Farms, and they
transferred to HelthWyzer together. After Snowman's
mother ran away, Ramona started dating Snowman's
father and eventually married him. Ramona cared
for Snowman like a mother, and though Snowman
appreciated her kindness, he also resented it. Ramona
continued to write to Snowman after he moved away,
describing her failed attempts to have a child with
his father.

Crake's Mother   Unnamed. Crake's mother worked a lot and left
her son to his own devices, though to Snowman it
appeared that she didn't care about Crake. Crake's
mother died a sudden, violent death after getting
exposed to a mysterious virus. Crake witnessed her
death, and Snowman later suspected that Crake had
something to do with it.

Crake's Father   Unnamed. Crake's father worked for HelthWyzer,
and he discovered that the company actively fabricated
new diseases, which it distributed through vitamin
pills. After Crake's father threatened to leak what he
knew to the media, the company executed him but
made it look like a suicide.

Uncle Pete   Crake's stepfather. Uncle Pete worked for
HelthWyzer, and he was the supervisor for the
division where Crake's father worked. He was a
friend of the family, which is why Crake called

him "uncle." After Crake's father died, Uncle Pete married Crake's mother and became his stepfather. Crake disliked Uncle Pete, and Snowman later suspected that Crake was behind Uncle Pete's sudden and mysterious death.

Uncle En   The businessman who first purchased Oryx. Uncle En bought children from the villages surrounding a major Asian city, then used those children in a variety of moneymaking schemes, such as selling flowers to tourists.

Jack   An American camera operator who worked in the child pornography industry. Jack befriended Oryx and taught her English in exchange for sexual favors.

Amanda Payne   Snowman's college girlfriend. Amanda was a conceptual artist who made large-scale installations. She used animal parts to spell out words in open outdoor spaces, and she filmed the action when birds of prey descended to "vulturize" her sculptures.

Bernice   Snowman's freshman-year suite mate. Bernice was a hardcore vegan and feminist who terrorized Snowman for eating meat and for having an active sex life.

Children of Crake   A tribe of genetically enhanced humans created by Crake. Also referred to as "Crakers," the Children of Crake represent a new subspecies of *Homo sapiens* that Crake designed to eliminate sexual competition and aggression. Crake outfitted the Children of Crake with genetic and behavioral features drawn from a variety of other animals. These features enable them to survive in the postapocalyptic world. Although they each have a name, Snowman has a hard time telling them apart due to a lack of distinguishing personality traits.

Abraham Lincoln The budding leader of the Children of Crake. Though each of the Crakers has a name based on a historical figure, Abraham Lincoln is the only one Snowman recognizes, because he frequently speaks on the Crakers' behalf. Crake wanted his new breed of humans to live in a nonhierarchical society that lacked leaders, and Snowman recognizes that Abraham Lincoln's leader-like qualities go against Crake's design.

CHARACTER LIST

Analysis of Major Characters

Snowman

Snowman is the protagonist of *Oryx and Crake*. The narrative recounts his life in the postapocalyptic present as well as in the preapocalyptic past. Snowman is perhaps the sole human survivor of a pandemic, and he is in charge of a tribe of genetically enhanced humans created by his friend-turned-rival, Crake. Although he takes responsibility for protecting the "Crakers," he also feels distant from them due to their childlike nature and superior genetic adaptations. As such, Snowman suffers a profound sense of loneliness, and when not scrounging for the resources he needs to survive, he spends much of his time immersed in memories of his old life. Snowman's early life, when he was called Jimmy, was largely shaped by his mother's abandonment of him, his friendship with the intelligent but unemotional Crake, and a growing fascination with sex. Snowman also felt scarred by his cold relationship with his father, who remained disappointed in Snowman's poor performance in math and science. Snowman did show an early gift for performance and wordplay, which earned him popularity among his high school peers. Even so, in a world increasingly dominated by science and technology, Snowman's affinity for language and the arts marked him as an antiquated and economically unviable throwback.

In the present time of the novel, Snowman journeys back to the Paradice facility at the RejoovenEsense Compound, where Crake developed the plague that obliterated the world's population. Snowman's main objective is to collect supplies, and throughout the journey he feels haunted by various memories and particularly by his mother's abandonment. He's also haunted by voices from his past, especially the voice of Oryx, a young woman he first saw on a child pornography website and later fell in love with. Other voices that float through Snowman's mind come from literature and other texts he read at university. More than anything, though, what haunts Snowman are memories of his longtime friendship with Crake. Snowman recalls the entire history of their relationship, from the time they met in high school, all the way through the period when they worked together at RejoovenEsense. Although the reader doesn't know the full extent of what Crake did until the end of the novel, Snowman's recollections throughout the book give a fragmentary account of how Crake came to create his disastrous plague. Snowman also frets about his own culpability, since he failed to see the signs indicating who Crake would become.

CRAKE

Crake was Snowman's best friend, a gifted scientist who eventually developed and released the catastrophic plague that ravaged the earth's human population. Crake's view of the world was coldly rational and fiercely atheistic. In addition to rejecting the idea of God, Crake also rejected the idea of capital-N "Nature," a quasi-divine notion that he believed encouraged a false distinction between what is natural and what is unnatural. During his undergraduate education at the elite Watson-Crick Institute, Crake developed an interest in and extraordinary gift for transgenic research. In contrast to Snowman, who struggled to see genetically modified creatures as natural or "real," Crake insisted that anything that could be imagined or created was real. Crake's strictly scientific approach to the world also linked to his sociopathic personality, which allowed him to pursue his ambitious genetic research without concern for the moral implications of that research. Snowman believes that Crake played an important role in the deaths of his own mother and stepfather, which provides further evidence that Crake may have been a sociopath.

Yet despite Crake's apparent sociopathic personality and his insistence on scientific rationalism, he remains all too human, afflicted by sexual desire, love, and maybe even jealousy—all of which he longed to eliminate from his new race of genetically enhanced humans. During his student days at Watson-Crick, Crake arranged sexual encounters through Student Services, and it was through one of these encounters that he met and fell in love with Oryx. His affection for Oryx led him to hire her as a member of the Paradice Project. At Paradice, Oryx started an affair with Snowman, and though Snowman worried that Crake would feel jealous, Oryx insisted that he was "too smart" for petty jealousy. Even so, Crake ended up slitting Oryx's throat, and Snowman shot Crake in response. Though Snowman cannot be certain about Crake's reasons for killing Oryx, he theorizes that jealousy may have played some role. If Snowman's theory is correct, then Crake's desire to create a new race of humans that doesn't exhibit any sexual competition has a certain tragic irony to it, since it implies that Crake wanted to quash behaviors to which he himself felt susceptible.

ORYX

Oryx is the mysterious young woman with whom both Snowman and Crake fall in love. Born in a rural village somewhere in south or southeast Asia, Oryx was sold into slavery at a young age and spent much of her early life working in the sex industry. Despite the numerous traumas of her youth, Oryx retained a positive attitude. Snowman and Crake first saw Oryx in a video on a child pornography site when they were teenagers. Later, when he was at college, Crake hired her for sexual services. They became lovers, and he employed her at RejoovenEsense, where she worked as a teacher for the Children of Crake. She seduced Snowman and became his lover as well. Despite their intimacy, Snowman never felt like he fully understood Oryx or her motivations. When he inquired about her past, she resisted discussing anything in detail. Only when pressed did she tell Snowman what she went through, but Snowman remained suspicious that she was just humoring him. Oryx remained a mystery to the end, and she largely functions in the novel as a symbol of the intellectual and, later, sexual rivalry between Snowman and Crake.

THEMES, MOTIFS & SYMBOLS

THEMES

Themes are the fundamental and often universal ideas explored in a literary work.

THE DANGER OF SCIENTIFIC ADVANCEMENT

The pre-apocalyptic world of *Oryx and Crake* was full of science and technology companies focused on transgenic research. In constantly pushing the boundaries of possibility, these companies eventually drove civilization over the edge. The term "transgenic research" refers to genetic research that involves artificially introducing genetic material from one species into the DNA of another species. Jimmy's father worked on transgenic research projects. For example, he was the chief architect of the pigoon, a hybrid pig creature that he designed to grow human kidneys as well as human skin cells. The novel also references a range of other hybrid creatures, like rakunks, wolvogs, bobkittens, and luminescent rabbits genetically altered with jellyfish DNA. Like Jimmy's father, Crake was a gifted researcher in the field of transgenics. He became so skilled, in fact, that early in his career he began developing his own projects and leading his own research facility. Crake's most impressive feats of engineering included the BlyssPluss pill and his new race of genetically enhanced humans. Like Crake, few researchers were concerned about the implications of their work at the time. However, from Snowman's perspective in the postapocalyptic present, it is clear that the lust for scientific advancement led directly to the end of civilization through giving power and resources to unscrupulous researchers.

THE DOMINANCE OF CORPORATE POWER

The society that Snowman grew up in was organized around corporations that wielded an unprecedented and dangerous amount of power. In the world represented in *Oryx and Crake*, corporations had become so powerful that they had reconfigured where and how people lived. In the twentieth century, people generally migrated toward urban centers. But as corporate power continued to rise throughout the twenty-first century, corporations moved out of the cities and established massive compounds that doubled as gated communities. Employees of these corporations lived in posh residential sectors with houses designed in a range of historic architectural styles. Corporate compounds also included movie theaters, malls, and other elements that once characterized middle-class suburban life but now belonged only to those privileged enough to have high-paying corporate jobs. The clearest example of the danger of corporate dominance appears at the end of the novel, when it becomes clear that the catastrophic event that killed most of the world's population originated at RejoovenEsense, a particularly powerful corporation with an especially luxurious compound. The enormous resources provided by RejoovenEsense enabled Crake to do the research and development necessary to execute his apocalyptic plan.

The Devaluation of Art

Oryx and Crake stages a symbolic battle between the sciences and the arts, with Crake representing the "science" side and Snowman representing the "art" side. In the pre-apocalyptic world of the novel, the sciences clearly dominated at the expense of the arts. All of the major corporations focused their vast financial and human resources on developing cutting-edge technologies and new lines of transgenic research. The corporate bias in favor of the sciences drove the economy as well as society at large. For this reason, schools placed a much greater emphasis on student success in their math and science coursework. When Crake and Jimmy were in high school, Crake won accolades for his natural abilities in math and science, whereas Jimmy, who got middling grades in his math and science classes, earned little more than his father's disappointment. The gap between the two boys grew after graduation, when Crake attended a well-funded science institute and Jimmy went to a crumbling humanities academy. Over the course of their friendship, Crake always enjoyed more privileges than Jimmy, and he also openly expressed an indifference to art. Crake's indifference gestures to the novel's overarching theme of the devaluation of art.

MOTIFS

Motifs are recurring structures, contrasts, or literary devices that can help to develop and inform the text's major themes.

VOICES

Throughout the chapters set in the present time, Snowman frequently hears voices in his head. All of the voices Snowman hears come from his past, and he can't seem to control them. Although these past voices sometimes keep him company in his otherwise lonely situation, their involuntary appearance in his head can sometimes make him feel haunted or tortured by his previous life. Some of the voices Snowman hears speak in quotes from literature or from the manuals and self-help textbooks that he studied for his undergraduate thesis. Even though Snowman remembers the words, he often forgets where the words come from and who wrote them. Snowman also occasionally has a difficult time identifying the other voices that belonged to real people he used to know. This inability to remember suggests that Snowman's memories of his old life are receding and may eventually leave him abandoned and all alone in the present. The voice that comes to him most frequently, and which Snowman has no trouble identifying, is that of Oryx. Before the apocalyptic event that devastated the world, Snowman was in love with this woman, and his continued preoccupation with her voice indicates just how desperate he feels for companionship now that he's alone.

MEMORY

Snowman spends much of his time dealing with the desperation of his present situation by thinking about his past. Memory is thus an important and ever-present motif, both in Snowman's thoughts and in the narrative structure, which constantly moves back and forth between the present and the past. Snowman recognizes that his preoccupation with the past prevents him from being more proactive about his own survival. In addition to misplacing useful tools, like the knife he once found and quickly lost, he has also proven to be an ineffective scavenger, often prioritizing his search for alcohol and forgetting to look for essentials like soap. In Chapter 3, Snowman tries to remind himself to focus on the present. He calls to mind the words from a survival manual that advised its reader to "avoid pointless repinings." The phrase "pointless repinings" comes back several times throughout the novel. Snowman's repetition of this phrase is ironic because even though his memories won't change anything, they do keep him company, and thus they may not be so pointless after all.

PLAYING GOD

At several points in the novel, Snowman draws attention to how Crake played God. Despite his resolute atheism, Crake cast himself as a symbolic God when he designed the facility named Paradice and populated it with a new breed of humans. Although Crake likely took an ironic attitude toward the name "Paradice," Snowman recognizes that Crake really did have a God complex. Not only did he create a new race of people, but he also took it upon himself to exterminate the existing human population. In the present time, Snowman twists Crake's irony against itself by turning Crake into a god to be worshipped by the Children of Crake. Snowman describes himself as the "God of Bullshit," and he makes up outlandish creation stories that the Crakers wholeheartedly believe. Effectively, Snowman has become Crake's prophet, and he is writing the liturgy for Crake's worship.

SYMBOLS

Symbols are objects, characters, figures, or colors used to represent abstract ideas or concepts.

BLOOD AND ROSES

Blood and Roses is the name of a game that Crake and Jimmy played when they were in high school and which pits humanity's greatest offenses ("blood") against humanity's greatest achievements ("roses"). Snowman recalls that it was always more difficult to play on the roses side, since there were far more examples of humanity's offenses, and in any case the spectacular and shocking nature of the "blood" events proved easier to remember. Although it's just a game from Snowman's past, Blood and Roses symbolizes the experience he is having in the present. Snowman is possibly the only survivor of a human-made plague that caused a devastating pandemic. Undoubtedly, Crake's plague counts as the most horrific example of a "blood" event in all of human history. Yet Snowman managed to survive the event, and against all odds, he continues to try to remember the few examples of human civilization that he can still feel proud of. In other words, Snowman is playing a real-life game of Blood and Roses, and although he knows it's much harder to win on the "roses" side, that side still does have a hand to play.

ALEX THE PARROT

Snowman first encountered Alex the Parrot when he was a boy, and this bird, which continues to come up in his thoughts and dreams, symbolizes Snowman's unfulfilled desire for meaningful companionship. Shortly after he started going to school, Snowman spent his extra time at lunch watching old instructional videos. One of his favorite videos featured a parrot named Alex who had to perform certain tasks involving a blue triangle and a yellow square. Snowman especially liked the part when Alex became annoyed with the researchers and said, "I'm going away now." Snowman's fascination with Alex made him want a parrot for his birthday. His parents were generally distant and unaffectionate, so his longing for a pet indicated a desire for companionship. Later, when Snowman returns to Paradice and sleeps in his old room there, he has a terrifying dream in which Alex the Parrot says "the blue triangle," and then announces his departure. Snowman cries out, "No, not yet," then wakes up. The fright Snowman experiences when Alex says he's leaving speaks to his abandonment issues, which primarily relate to his mother, but also to the now-dead Crake and Oryx. The blue triangle in the dream references their broken love triangle.

THE CHILDREN OF ORYX

According to the mythology of the Children of Crake, all plant and animal life are counted among the "Children of Oryx." The Crakers have been taught to respect the Children of Oryx. In order to avoid harming any animals under Oryx's protection, the Crakers maintain a strict vegetarian diet. And whenever one of the Children of Oryx harms one of the Children of Crake, the Crakers pray in order to calm Oryx's anger. The Crakers' respect for the Children of Oryx recalls pagan nature cults that have existed for centuries, and which understood all animals and plants to be inhabited by some kind of spirit or energy. Such a belief would clearly be alien to the pre-apocalyptic world of Oryx and Crake, in which no plant or animal is sacred. On the contrary, scientists feel entitled to mix and match plant and animal DNA on a whim, mostly for the purposes of scientific research but sometimes just for fun. The reverence the Crakers display for the Children of Oryx therefore symbolizes the resurrection of an earlier form of respect for the earth that has the capacity to help the environmentally devastated planet begin to heal.

SYMBOLS

Summary & Analysis

Epigraphs & Chapter 1

Summary

Oryx and Crake begins with a pair of epigraphs from literary sources. The first epigraph comes from Jonathan Swift's 1726 novel *Gulliver's Travels*. In this passage, Swift's narrator claims that he will not astonish his reader with "strange improbable tales," but rather relate his story "in the simplest manner and style." The second epigraph comes from Virginia Woolf's 1927 novel *To the Lighthouse*. This passage consists of three questions, each of which asks about how to navigate through the dangerous "ways of the world."

The novel proper opens with a man named Snowman waking up just before dawn. He can hear the rhythms of waves, which are crashing into large piles of rusting cars and rubble that have accumulated on the beach. Snowman climbs down from the tree and walks to a hidden cache where he stores food and other supplies. Before eating his last mango, he recites a quote to himself. He doesn't know where the words come from, but they make him think of European colonialism.

Later that morning, Snowman observes a group of naked people playing on the beach, collecting pieces of flotsam that have washed up on shore. Although Snowman refers to these people as the Children of Crake, they are, in fact, mostly adults. Snowman reflects on the differences between these "children" and himself. For example, they are resistant to UV light, whereas he must hide from the sun. Snowman wonders whether his attitude toward the Children of Crake is one of envy or nostalgia.

Snowman reflects on his name, which he based on the "Abominable Snowman." The name brings him pleasure for the way it violates a rule that a person named Crake once made about selecting a name. Crake said that "no name could be chosen for which a physical equivalent . . . could not be demonstrated."

Some of the Children of Crake come to Snowman and ask about his beard. Snowman replies that he's growing feathers. Unlike him, the Children of Crake have bare faces.

Later, on the beach, Snowman speaks aloud to himself: "All, all alone. Alone on a wide, wide sea." Snowman reflects on his desire to hear another human voice, and soon thereafter he hears the voice of a woman in his ear, an echo from his past. He can't figure out which woman the voice belongs to, but he suspects it might belong to a prostitute, since she's commenting on his "nice abs." This isn't the voice Snowman wants to hear. He begins to cry, and his chest feels tight. He screams at the ocean, cursing Crake and blaming him for the current state of the world: "You did this!" Snowman waits for an answer that doesn't come. He wipes tears from his face and tells himself, "Get a life."

ANALYSIS

Each of the epigraphs to *Oryx and Crake* offers a different way to frame the narrative to come. The first epigraph comes from *Gulliver's Travels*, a novel by Jonathan Swift that follows the character Lemuel Gulliver through his improbable journeys to four very strange lands. Despite the fantastical nature of Gulliver's experiences, he claims that his main aim was to educate rather than simply amuse the reader. As such, he composed his travelogue in a plain style meant to indicate the truth of what he went through. Though clearly a work of fiction, Swift had Gulliver attest to the truth of his travels in order to suggest to his readers that fiction, though strictly made up, may nonetheless have true things to say about the world. Atwood's use of this passage from *Gulliver's Travels* suggests that though the events recounted in Oryx and Crake are fictional, they have something to say about where the "real" world might be headed. In other words, though Atwood has not based her novel on a true story, the events depicted in the novel could nonetheless become true in the future.

Atwood's second epigraph comes from Virginia Woolf's novel *To the Lighthouse*, and taken as a whole, it asks what a person should do if they lack guidance, shelter, and a basic sense of safety. As the reader will find out, the sense of chaos and lack of control conjured in this epigraph applies well to the character Snowman, who may be the sole survivor of a catastrophic event and now has nothing to guide his existence in a postapocalyptic world. In addition to this thematic significance, the Woolf epigraph also signals something important about the narrative structure of *Oryx and Crake*. Woolf's novel is famous for taking place in two different times, ten years apart from one another. Similarly, Atwood's novel follows two different narratives that take place at different times. Specifically, the novel tells of Snowman's experiences in the present time as well as Snowman's past. The epigraph from *To the Lighthouse* thus also indicates an important relationship between past and present in *Oryx and Crake*.

The novel proper opens on a postapocalyptic world where the sun poses a serious hazard and the ocean crashes against piles of rusting junk. Though the reader does not yet have any details about what events led to the current situation, we find numerous references to past events in the thoughts of the protagonist, Snowman. Snowman's most emotionally intense thoughts point to a person named Crake. Crake clearly had something to do with whatever happened. Based on the differences between Snowman and the Children of Crake, the reader can infer that the Children are the products of some kind of genetic experiments, and that Crake may have been the scientist who spearheaded those experiments. Even so, it remains unclear what the Children of Crake might have to do with the current state of the world. The fragmentary nature of Snowman's thoughts helps build suspense by presenting partial information that the narrative to come promises to complete.

In addition to his thoughts about Crake, Snowman hears voices from the past that constantly remind him of his loneliness. The voices indicate that Snowman feels preoccupied with the life he has lost and maybe even haunted by his memories of that life. Aside from the voices of others, Snowman talks to himself. Some of what Snowman says aloud comes from books he once read, though he can't seem to remember what they were. For example, he recites: "It is the strict adherence to daily routine that tends toward the maintenance of good morale and the preservation of sanity." These words come from Kurt Vonnegut's novel about time travel, *Slaughterhouse-Five*. Later, when he says the words "All, all alone," Snowman is quoting a line from the British Romantic poet Samuel Coleridge's "Rime of the Ancient Mariner." Both Vonnegut's novel and Coleridge's poem concern individuals struggling to navigate desperate situations, much like Snowman, and their inclusion in the first chapter sets the stage for a tense and stark tale.

CHAPTER 2

SUMMARY

The narrative moves back in time and recounts Snowman's memories of his childhood, when his name was Jimmy. Snowman recalls

his earliest memory, when he was five and a half years old and witnessed a massive bonfire of animal carcasses. Snowman's mind links
this memory of a bonfire to another memory of when he burned his
own hair, which caused a fight between his parents.

Snowman's mind returns to the bonfire, and he recalls how, as
Jimmy, he felt culpable for all the animals who died since he hadn't
done anything to save them. He also recalls some confusion around
what was happening and why, though in retrospect it seems clear
that the bonfire was related to some kind of virus. The day after the
fire, Jimmy asked his parents why the animals had to be burned. His
father answered that they had to be burned to prevent the spread
of disease. His father also joked that Jimmy might have caught the
disease, which angered his mother.

The narrator explains that Jimmy's father was an employee at
OrganInc Farms, where he worked as a "genographer"—that is,
someone who maps genetic material. His father rose to prominence
at OrganInc Farms for helping design the "pigoon," a pig-like animal that served as a transgenic host for up to six human kidneys.
When the kidneys were mature, they could be transplanted to human
hosts, all without harming the pigoon, which would survive to grow
another crop of kidneys. The pigoons were kept secure in special
buildings where Jimmy used to visit them.

One day in the OrganInc cafeteria Jimmy overheard a conversation between his father and his colleague Ramona. They talked about
Jimmy's mother, Sharon, and her battle with depression. Ramona
lamented that Jimmy's mother used to be so smart. The narrator
explains that Jimmy's mother previously worked as a microbiologist at OrganInc Farms. She told Jimmy that she left her job to stay
at home with him, but he felt suspicious, since she left her job just
when he started going to school. Jimmy's mother had frequent mood
swings, and Jimmy desired to make her feel better.

Jimmy lived with his family in a suburb-like area called the
Modules, which was the residential portion of the larger OrganInc
Farms Compound. Everything in the Compound was designed to
replicate the comfortable lifestyle of a previous generation. The
Compound featured replica homes built in older architectural
styles, as well as pools, shopping malls, restaurants, and more. The
Compound kept OrganInc Farms families sequestered from the outside, and particularly from the increasingly lawless and dangerous
cities, known as "pleeblands."

Jimmy's father appreciated the protection offered by the Compound, and he compared the Compound's function to that of a castle. Like the Compound, "Castles were for keeping you and your buddies nice and safe inside, and for keeping everybody else outside." By contrast, Jimmy's mother complained that the Compound was little more than "a theme park," and she insisted that no matter how much the designers tried to replicate earlier standards of living, they "could never bring the old ways back."

Analysis

Chapter 2 makes a transition from the narrative of Snowman, which takes place in the present, to the narrative of Jimmy, which takes place in the past. Although they have different names, Snowman and Jimmy are in fact the same person. Snowman thinks of his younger self as a different person, and the narrative therefore treats Jimmy as Snowman's alter ego. The distinction between "Jimmy" and "Snowman" has two functions in the novel. On a practical level, it clarifies when the narrative takes place in the past versus the present. On a thematic level, it emphasizes the significance of the apocalyptic event that radically transformed the world. Looking back on his past from his postapocalyptic perspective, Snowman recognizes that a gulf of experience separates his present self from the person he was before the event. Put differently, Jimmy could be said to have died in the apocalypse and given birth to a new self: Snowman.

The world that Jimmy lived in differed greatly from the world Snowman currently lives in. In Jimmy's world, corporations that specialized in science and technology had a tremendous amount of power. In fact, such corporations had so much power that they created new social hierarchies between people who worked in the science-and-technology sector and those who did not. This social hierarchy also mapped onto the landscape. Whereas those employed by powerful corporations lived and worked in affluent and well-protected areas known as Compounds, others had to survive in the increasingly dangerous and derelict cities, known as "pleeblands," after the word plebeian, which means "commoners." Jimmy's family lived in the OrganInc Farms Compound, and his parents had divergent opinions about the quality of their life there. Jimmy's father represents a compliant, corporate attitude, as he defended the Compound system, and affirmed the importance of keeping the social elite separate from the riffraff of the pleeblands.

By contrast, Jimmy's mother gives a rebellious perspective, as she found the Compound system stifling and sterile and longed for a more authentic way of living.

The question of "authenticity" also extends to the issue of genetic engineering. In Chapter 2, the reader learns that Jimmy's father played a key role in developing the pigoon, a genetically modified pig-like creature designed to grow human kidneys. Although the pigoons were not designed to be slaughtered for food, as climate change began to alter the environment and the OrganInc Farms cafeteria served more and more bacon, employees joked that they were, in fact, eating pigoon meat. Despite being presented as a humorous rumor, the employees' inability to tell the difference between genetically modified bacon and the "real" thing has an important thematic resonance. The rumor about pigoon bacon points to a larger thematic question about whether or not the new "bioforms" manufactured by corporate scientists could be considered natural and whether it matters if no one can even tell the difference between natural and unnatural.

Another important theme that arises in Chapter 2 relates to Jimmy's relationship with his mother, who grew increasingly depressed after leaving her job as a microbiologist at OrganInc Farms. When Jimmy was very young, he had an unusually intense attachment to his mother. The intensity of Jimmy's attachment created confusion when he witnessed his mother's depressive episodes. He identified so strongly with his mother that he could no longer separate their emotions, and he confused her sadness with his own. As the reader will see later in the novel, the emotional confusion Jimmy experienced early on in his relationship with his mother set the groundwork for the complex and at times tortured feelings he would develop toward her later in life. Jimmy's early emotional confusion about his mother provides a foundation for all of Jimmy's future relationships with women.

CHAPTER 3

SUMMARY

Strange to think of the endless labour, the digging, the hammering, the carving, the lifting, the drilling, day by day, year by year, century by century; and now the

endless crumbling that must be going on everywhere.
Sandcastles in the wind.

(See QUOTATIONS, p. 63)

The narrative returns to the present, with Snowman retreating into the forest as the heat of noon approaches. He goes to lie down on a bed he's made in the shade of the forest. Snowman recalls that the lean-to he originally erected didn't offer him adequate protection from the sun's dangerous UV rays. Because he built the lean-to at ground level, he also had to deal with ants as well as pigoons and rakunks (a genetic splice of raccoon and skunk).

The word *Mesozoic* randomly comes to Snowman's mind, but he can't remember what it means. He mourns the fact that he's forgetting more and more of "the entries on his cherished wordlists." As he lies in bed, he hears the voice of an old schoolteacher. Snowman rebukes himself for his wandering thoughts and tells himself he needs to find a better use for his time. He thinks about whittling a chess set, which makes him think of when he used to play chess and other games with Crake. Snowman also considers finding pen and paper to keep a diary like a castaway, but he dismisses the idea since anyone who might read his diary is already dead.

Snowman observes a caterpillar descending on a thread, and he experiences a sudden, "inexplicable surge of tenderness and joy." But the moment of "irrational happiness" passes quickly, and Snowman says aloud to the caterpillar: "We are not here to play, to dream, to drift. . . . We have hard work to do, and loads to lift." Snowman wonders to himself where these words came from, and he thinks of the man who taught his junior high Life Skills class.

Snowman dismisses this memory, and his mind returns to the question of how to occupy his time. He thinks he should focus on improving his living conditions. He fantasizes about finding a cool, well-ventilated cave, and then he thinks about a nearby stream with fresh water that collects into a pool he likes to cool off in. He rejects the thought of going to the pool for fear that the "Crakers"—that is, the Children of Crake—might be there. He fears that they would encourage him to swim with them, and he doesn't want them to see him naked.

He falls into a half-sleep and has a dream of someone named Oryx wearing an elaborate dress and floating in a swimming pool. In the dream, he senses they are both in danger, and he hears a large, hollow boom. Snowman wakes up to thunder and wind and takes shelter. When the rain slows he goes to a collapsed bridge where he bathes and drinks runoff water.

Snowman suddenly feels overcome by the sensation of being trapped like a caged animal, and the thought makes him weep. Words from "the book in his head" come to mind, instructing him like a survival manual: "It is important . . . to ignore minor irritants, to avoid pointless repinings, and to turn one's mental energies to immediate realities and to the tasks at hand." He says the phrase "pointless repinings" aloud and wonders if someone might be listening.

ANALYSIS

Chapter 3 showcases the wandering nature of Snowman's mind, which moves from one thought or recollection to the next in a fragmentary way. Snowman feels preoccupied with his past and with his present situation, and his busy mind prevents him from giving adequate attention to his survival. But even when Snowman repudiates himself for being so self-involved, his scolding frequently leads to other thoughts and memories. For instance, as he moves into the forest he chastises himself for losing the pocketknife he had when he set up his first shelter near the beach. This moment of chastisement leads to a recollection of when his father gave him a similar knife on his ninth birthday. This memory brings forth yet another, when he told Oryx about the knife his father gave him. Snowman's busy mind signals the volatility of his overall emotional state, exemplified once again when his joy at seeing a caterpillar dissipates just as suddenly as it arises.

Snowman's emotional volatility separates him from the Children of Crake, who have an energetic but simple-minded sense of curiosity about the world. In contrast to Snowman, they show no traces of existential anguish. The Crakers also possess a childlike disposition that keeps them from feeling self-conscious. Snowman, on the other hand, chooses not to bathe at the river for fear of showing his naked body to the others, which would only make him feel "deformed." The gulf that separates Snowman from the Crakers has a profoundly alienating effect. Snowman even has a difficult time considering the Crakers to be fully human, even though they mostly look human. Despite not technically being alone in this postapocalyptic world, Snowman very much feels alone, isolated like an animal in a cage. Occasionally, Snowman's feelings of isolation and loneliness leave him feeling helpless and desperate.

It is precisely in order to avoid his feelings of hopelessness and desperation that Snowman turns his mind to the past. At the end of the chapter, after Snowman's sense of being trapped brings him to tears, he tries to calm himself by summoning words from an old survival manual that he once read. The words of the manual insist on the need to focus on immediate needs and "avoid pointless repinings"—that is, not think about useless memories. On the one hand, Snowman calls these words to mind in an effort to steady himself and get himself to focus on his own survival. On the other hand, the quote is ironic, since the words are themselves products of Snowman's memory, and hence examples of the "pointless repinings" he's instructing himself to avoid. As this example demonstrates, no matter how hard he tries, Snowman keeps getting sucked back into his recollections in order to avoid the difficulties of his present situation.

In addition to the words from the survival manual, Snowman also references other quotes and texts from his past. For instance, after his experience of joy with the caterpillar, he chastises himself with another quote that instructs him not to play, dream, or drift, but rather to do hard work. Snowman can't remember the source of the quote, which, in fact, comes from the hymn "Be Strong!" by the early-twentieth-century clergyman Maltbie Davenport Babcock. But despite his inability to remember the source, Snowman uses the quote as a resource for getting him through his current difficulty, much as he does with the quote from the survival manual. Yet Snowman's failure to remember the source also has significance since it indicates how his memory is beginning to fade. Just as he can't remember Babcock's name, he also can't remember the meaning of certain words, like "Mesozoic," that populated some kind of wordlist he once cherished. Snowman clearly relies on his memories of the past to get him through the present, but the fading of his memories indicates that he might be losing his grip on the past.

CHAPTER 4

SUMMARY

When did the body first set out on its own adventures? Snowman thinks; after having ditched its old travelling companions, the mind and the soul, for whom it had once been considered a mere corrupt vessel or else a

*puppet acting out their dramas for them, or else bad
company, leading the other two astray.*

(See QUOTATIONS, p. 63)

Snowman notices a rakunk nearby. He imagines taming the raccoon–
skunk hybrid in order to have someone to talk to. The narrative
then shifts to Jimmy's tenth birthday, when his father gave him a pet
rakunk that he named Killer.

Shortly after Jimmy's tenth birthday, the company NooSkins
headhunted his father. The family moved to the HelthWyzer
Compound, which was bigger and more luxurious than OrganInc
Farms. Jimmy's mother again expressed her discontent at feeling
like a prisoner.

One night Jimmy's father came home from work wanting to celebrate a breakthrough in his new project, which entailed using pigoons to grow human skin cells. Jimmy's mother refused to celebrate
and instead criticized her husband's work as morally reprehensible.

Several years passed, and Jimmy grew increasingly detached from
his parents. His only companion at home remained Killer.

One day Jimmy came home to find a note from his mother. She
had run away, and before she left she destroyed her husband's computer. She also abducted Killer, whom she planned to release into the
wild. Jimmy didn't know whether he mourned the loss of his mother
or his pet rakunk more.

In the aftermath of her departure, CorpSeCorps agents interrogated Jimmy regarding his mother's whereabouts. He claimed not to
know anything, even though he received cryptic postcards from an
"Aunt Monica" that clearly came from his mother.

After some time, Jimmy's father began dating his colleague
Ramona, and she moved in. Jimmy felt more alone and invisible than
ever. Eventually, though, Ramona extended Jimmy an olive branch,
and the two developed a cold but functional relationship.

In the present Snowman tells himself, "I am not my childhood,"
and he instructs himself not to forget his collection of words.

The narrative then moves back to a few months before Jimmy's
mother left, when a boy named Crake started at HelthWyzer High
School. (Crake's real name was Glenn, but Snowman claims that
he can only think of him as Crake.) Jimmy showed Crake around
on his first day of school, and he felt intrigued by Crake's quiet and
mysterious air. The two quickly became friends, hanging out after
school and playing a variety of games.

One of the games they played was called Blood and Roses, which weighed human atrocities against human achievements. Another game the boys played was Extinctathon, an online trivia game about extinct animal species monitored by a figure named MaddAddam. Crake became especially obsessed with this game, and he played under the codename "Crake," after an extinct Australian bird, the Red-Necked Crake.

When not playing games, Jimmy and Crake explored the dark side of the internet, including sites that streamed live video of surgeries, animal torture, executions, assisted suicides, and graphic sexual acts. One afternoon the boys logged on to a site called HottTotts, which featured tourists filming themselves engaged in sex acts that would be illegal in their home countries.

The narrator then explains that the two boys first saw Oryx on this site in a video that featured three young girls licking whipped cream off the body of a man. One of the girls looked straight into the camera, and Jimmy felt like she was making eye contact with him. Moved by the experience, he froze the frame and printed a copy of the screenshot.

The narrative moves forward to a time when Jimmy and Oryx were together. Jimmy showed her the image he'd printed out and asked her what she was thinking when she looked into the camera, but she responded evasively.

ANALYSIS

As Snowman's encounter with a rakunk leads him back to memories of his childhood pet, the reader begins to see that feelings of loneliness and isolation afflicted Snowman long before his current situation. Snowman recalls that neither of his parents ever really remembered his birthday or how old he was turning. His mother was out of touch and gave age-inappropriate presents. Meanwhile, his father always forgot about his birthday but then turned around and gave him a big present the day after to make up for forgetting. This pattern repeated on Snowman's tenth birthday, and his father brought home the pet rakunk named Killer. Even though Killer provided some degree of companionship and comfort, the rakunk also symbolized the degree to which Snowman's parents remained distant and inattentive. Snowman's loneliness only grew more acute in subsequent years, and particular after his mother left with Killer in tow. The loneliness that traumatized Snowman in his youth clearly continues to affect him in the present, when Snowman tries to convince his adult self that he is not his childhood.

The most traumatic experience of Snowman's youth was his mother's sudden departure. Snowman felt deeply attached to his mother when he was a boy, so when she left him, he felt abandoned and betrayed. Though he missed his mother and felt her absence intensely, those emotions also became mixed up with feelings of resentment, which led to deep psychological confusion. In addition to representing a defining moment in Snowman's life, his mother's departure also signals an important theme in the novel regarding genetic research, the moral implications of which troubled his mother. The conversation that Snowman overheard between his parents makes it clear that his mother left her own job at OrganInc Farms because she no longer believed that the research such companies pursued was morally defensible. Her critical stance on genetic engineering foreshadows her involvement with God's Gardeners, an activist group that protests all research into genetic manipulation.

The troubling activities Jimmy and Crake engaged in have important implications for how their personalities develop in the rest of the novel. Although Jimmy felt disturbed by much of the sexual and violent video content they watched, nothing seemed to affect Crake. Crake's lack of an emotional response may suggest that he had a sociopathic personality, meaning that he couldn't understand what others were feeling. In addition to watching graphic videos, the boys also played a range of games. Crake obsessively mastered every game he and Jimmy played, which demonstrated a compulsiveness always to be the best. The content of the games the boys played also has significance. Blood and Roses warrants special mention here since the game staged a battle between the achievements of human civilization and examples of human barbarity. In the present time, Snowman recalls that it was always difficult to win on the "Roses" side, since it was much easier to remember "the Blood stuff." This observation reflects the reality of Snowman's present situation, as he tries to save the words on his wordlist from extinction in the wake of a human-driven apocalypse. The "Blood stuff" appears to have prevailed.

Just as Chapter 4 recounts how Crake first came into Jimmy's life, it also recounts how Jimmy and Crake first encountered Oryx while surfing a child pornography website. Jimmy instantly felt transfixed by the little girl who gazed directly at the camera. Her direct eye contact stirred him emotionally and made him feel both desire and shame. He felt desire because he found her attractive. Yet he also felt shame because her gaze seemed to call him out and chastise him for watching such morally repulsive material. Up until this moment Jimmy didn't register that watching child pornography might be immoral, but her gaze made him question his own actions. Although Jimmy didn't realize it at the time, Oryx's gaze also had a profound effect on Crake, who would also hold on to the screenshot image. The fact that both Jimmy and Crake felt attached to Oryx the moment they first saw her will have important implications later in the novel.

CHAPTER 5

SUMMARY

In the present time, Snowman sits on the edge of the tree line at dusk, feeling dejected and hungry. He observes light passing through unbroken windowpanes submerged underwater and looks at overgrown rooftop gardens on abandoned buildings. He also notices a foraging rabbit with huge teeth and a semi-translucent glow, evidently the product of interbreeding between wild rabbits and the "luminous green rabbits" that had been developed in labs.

Snowman wants to hunt the rabbit for food, but then recalls that, according to the Children of Crake's beliefs, rabbits "belong to the Children of Oryx and are sacred to Oryx herself." He decides against killing the rabbit lest he upset the vegetarian Crakers. He then recalls the origin story that he'd made up for the Children of Crake and reminds himself of the importance of internal consistency in storytelling.

Stars begin to appear, and to himself Snowman recites the nursery rhyme that starts, "Star light, star bright." He recites more of the nursery rhyme aloud, but in response to the idea of making a wish, he thinks to himself, "Fat chance."

The Children of Crake appear and ask Snowman questions. A female voice comes into his head, instructing that "when dealing with indigenous peoples . . . you must attempt to respect their traditions and confine your explanations to simple concepts that can be understood within the contexts of their belief systems." Snowman dismisses the condescending voice and tells the Crakers they should stop asking questions or else they would "be toast." Snowman recognizes that he's made a slip using such an arcane metaphor. He imagines all the other difficult-to-answer questions that would arise if he actually tried to explain what toast is.

As the sky darkens Snowman thinks about the names of oil paints, and he comments that all words and phrases are fantasies, though they are also signs of human ingenuity. He reflects that Crake did not have a high opinion of human ingenuity.

Snowman sees a group of Crakers approaching. The women present Snowman with a grilled fish, which is a ritual they perform weekly based on a story Snowman made up about Oryx. Though the Children of Crake are all vegetarians, they accept his eating habits and believe his story about Oryx.

The Crakers gather closer and ask Snowman to tell them about the deeds of Crake. Snowman launches into a rehearsed origin story: "In the beginning, there was chaos." He explains that all the people in the world were full of chaos, killing each other and eating the Children of Oryx. Then Crake banished the chaos through the Great Rearrangement, which made the Great Emptiness. The Crakers ask Snowman to tell them how Crake was born, and Snowman explains that Crake was never born, but rather "he came down out of the sky."

The Children of Crake go away, and Snowman climbs into his tree with a bottle of Scotch from his cache and drinks the remaining alcohol as a pack of wolvogs assembles on the ground. He finishes the Scotch and throws the bottle down at them.

Snowman looks up at the stars and thinks again about the nursery rhyme. Later he imagines a hand touching him, and he masturbates while fantasizing about Oryx.

ANALYSIS

In this chapter the reader continues to learn about Snowman's personality and his ongoing struggle to cope with his situation. Snowman exhibits a struggle between earnestness and cynicism. For example, he reclines in his tree, looking at the stars and reciting the nursery rhyme about making a wish on the first star that appears in the sky. He then quickly dismisses his own nostalgia with cynicism, telling himself "fat chance." And yet Snowman circles back around to the nursery rhyme at the end of the chapter, suggesting that a part of him really does want to make a wish, even if he knows it won't make a difference. Aside from the play of earnestness and cynicism, this chapter also showcases how Snowman uses alcohol and sex to cope with his present situation.

For example, as he fetches the last bottle of Scotch in his cache, Snowman recalls that immediately after the event, he scavenged abandoned bars and homes for alcohol and got drunk every night. In addition to managing his emotions with alcohol, Snowman also copes by thinking about sex, as when, at the end of the chapter, he indulges in a sexual fantasy about Oryx.

As Snowman interacts more with the Children of Crake, the reader also learns more about the genetic and cultural differences that separate Snowman from the Crakers. The Crakers all have perfectly formed bodies modeled on the images that used to be propagated by the advertising industry. The Crakers also have luminescent green eyes that, similar to the genetically modified rabbits, glow because of some jellyfish DNA. These details give the reader more information about what makes the Crakers so different. Whereas the genetic differences make Snowman feel like the Crakers belong to a different species, he also sees the difference as a cultural one and treats the Crakers as if they belong to a primitive tribe. For example, when the Crakers first approach him in this chapter, Snowman recalls words from an old anthropology text. The words instruct him to use culturally appropriate metaphors when communicating with "indigenous peoples," and he dismisses the voice in his head as condescending. However, he quickly recognizes the truth of the anthropological text when he uses "toast" as a metaphor and realizes how much confusion it could cause if he tried to explain what toast is.

Despite the fact that Snowman must choose his words carefully around the Crakers, he has clearly spent much of his time with them filling their heads with tales about Crake and the origin of the world. Snowman has made up these tales himself, creating a new mythology that mixes up elements from biblical stories, Greek fables, and Norse legends. The mythology Snowman has invented demonstrates his ingenuity as a storyteller. It also indicates Snowman's desire to interfere with Crake's legacy. As Snowman recalls, Crake strictly rejected all notions of God and divinity, and Snowman relishes the irony of feeding the Children of Crake fictions about their godlike creator. At the same time, Snowman resents the story he's made up, since it was he, and not Crake, who looked after the Crakers and kept them safe after the apocalyptic event. Furthermore, by deifying Crake, Snowman has unintentionally positioned himself as Crake's servant by becoming the man's prophet.

CHAPTER 6

SUMMARY
Snowman wakes up suddenly in the night. He hears an owl hooting, which conjures memories of Oryx. Snowman ponders Oryx's mysterious nature, and he wonders how long it took him to piece together an understanding of Oryx from the fragments of information he gathered about her.

The narrative shifts to the past and begins to recount Oryx's life story. She was born in a rural village somewhere in Asia, although she doesn't remember exactly where. Most families in the village were poor, and Oryx's family was no exception. In order to make ends meet, families often sold one or more of their children to a businessman named Uncle En from the city, who would take them away and claimed to employ them as flower sellers. This fate befell Oryx, who, along with a brother, was sold to Uncle En.

Oryx, her brother, and two other children traveled with Uncle En from the village to an unknown city, the chaos of which shocked the children. Once they arrived at their destination, Uncle En confined the newcomers in a room with other children, who related stories about their experiences.

Soon after their arrival Uncle En taught Oryx and the other newcomers how to sell flowers to tourists. Oryx had a natural gift for the work. She was small and fragile, and because she looked like an "angelic doll" she had no problem selling her daily quota. However, her doll-like appearance also put her in danger of sexual predators, and one day a man asked her to come with him to his hotel. She refused and reported the encounter to Uncle En. He responded that that if another man asked her to accompany him, she should say yes. The next time a man approached Oryx, she followed him back to his hotel, where he removed his clothes and coaxed her to touch him. At this point Uncle En burst into the hotel room, and the man, mortified at having been caught, paid Uncle En a large sum of money. Oryx and Uncle En began to run this scam regularly.

One day a new man appeared claiming to have purchased Uncle En's flower business, though Oryx later learned that Uncle En had been murdered and thrown in a canal. The new man sold Oryx to a man who made child pornography. Later, Oryx told Jimmy about the men who paid to have themselves filmed with the girls, and she explained that her experiences taught her a valuable life lesson: "That everything has a price."

The man who operated the camera was named Jack, and he referred to the movie studio as "Pixieland," after all the young girls. Jack occasionally snuck the girls forbidden cigarettes, and he also coaxed Oryx into performing sexual favors in exchange for English lessons. Jimmy had a strong negative reaction to Oryx's story about Jack, and he pressed her for more details about what Jack and the other men did to her. Oryx resisted Jimmy's questions and said, "We should think only beautiful things." Jimmy rejected Oryx's "sweetness and acceptance and crap" and insisted that her experiences must have traumatized her.

Analysis

Although Oryx has already come up many times in previous chapters, Chapter 6 provides the first substantial insight into who she is and where she came from. As the chapter recounts, Oryx went through a number of difficult experiences. In addition to being sold to a mysterious man at an early age, she was also forced into sex work when she was still a young girl. These experiences forced Oryx to grow up quickly, and they also taught her important lessons about the world. In particular, she learned about the power of money to fulfill desire as well as money's ability to reduce human beings to commodities. While working for a child pornographer, she witnessed how the men who paid for the films could do anything they wanted as long as they had enough cash. Seeing this, Oryx learned that everything has a price, a lesson she would later recount to Jimmy. Furthermore, as a slave in the sex industry, Oryx realized that her whole existence had been reduced to monetary value. Having been wrenched away from her family and then separated from her brother, Oryx learned another lesson: "A money value was no substitute for love."

Throughout Chapter 6, the narrative moves between the account of Oryx's past and a later conversation between Oryx and Jimmy in which Jimmy questioned Oryx about her traumatic experiences. Jimmy clearly cared for Oryx, but his aggressive and invasive interrogation demonstrated an emotional immaturity and a warped sense of romantic love. Although it isn't clear why Jimmy was so fixated on Oryx's trauma, one possibility is that he wanted to connect with Oryx over his own traumatic experiences. Although Jimmy fixated on his own terrible childhood, Oryx refused to dwell on the dark parts of her past and instead insisted, "We should think only beautiful things." This demonstrates that Oryx had a fundamentally different approach to life than Jimmy. Whereas Jimmy believed that Oryx was hiding something from him, or else repressing her trauma, Oryx really did focus on the positive. For example, Oryx took it as a sign of her mother's love that she sold Oryx and her brother together so that they could keep each other company. It may seem terrible that their mother would sell either of them, but Oryx prefers to see evidence of love in a desperate choice.

In addition to providing the first information about Oryx's background, Chapter 6 also offers the first reference to a triangular relationship between Oryx, Crake, and Jimmy. When Jimmy pressed Oryx to admit that Jack took advantage of her, she responded by telling him that his behavior merely confirmed Crake's assessment that Jimmy lacked an "elegant mind." Oryx's revelation that she and Crake spoke about him behind his back disturbed Jimmy. Not only did it incite feelings of jealousy, but it also humiliated him to think that both Oryx and Crake saw him as intellectually deficient. Jimmy had long felt inferior, initially because of his father's ill treatment when he didn't show a knack for math and science, and later because Crake proved himself a genius in both math and science and went on to study at a much more prestigious university. The reference to Jimmy's inelegant mind therefore reignited his old feelings of shame, made worse because he also felt betrayed by both his friend and his lover.

CHAPTER 7

SUMMARY

Snowman wakes up hungover from his night of drinking. He climbs down from his tree to begin his daily routine, feeling vertigo both from his hangover and from his mixed-up thoughts about past, present, and future. He eats his last can of Sveltana No-Meat Cocktail Sausages and thinks about the need to find more food. He recalls that he used to be able to find fruit at a nearby arboretum, but the orchards there have since been thoroughly picked over. Snowman also contemplates raiding bird nests for eggs and hunting pigoons, but both options present difficulties, so he rejects them.

The idea comes to him to return to the Paradice facility in the RejoovenEsense Compound, where he believes there may still be a stock of supplies. However, the Compound is far away, and

Snowman knows the trip there and back will take at least two days. He begins to make his preparations, and then he sets off toward the Children of Crake to tell them about his plans.

When Snowman arrives, the male Crakers are performing their morning ritual, in which they form a circle around the village and urinate. Crake genetically programmed the men with the ability to mark territory with a strong scent that repels predators like wolvogs.

The men finish their ritual and invite Snowman into their circle, at the center of which a group of adults is taking care of a little boy injured from a bobkitten bite. The adults purr over the child, and Snowman recalls that Crake genetically equipped the Crakers with the capacity to purr at a particular frequency that promotes healing. The adults explain that they had to fend the bobkitten off with rocks and that they plan to apologize to Oryx later for harming one of her children. Snowman wonders whether the Crakers are developing religious sensibilities.

Snowman informs the Crakers of his plans to set out on a longer journey than usual. When Snowman tells them that he's going to see Crake, the Crakers express their desire to accompany Snowman and meet their creator. But Snowman insists that they stay where they are, and as he returns to his tree, he feels vexed about their misplaced gratitude toward Crake.

Snowman sets off on his journey, walking through former parkland with the sounds of bobkittens in the distance. He reflects that bobkittens had been introduced to control the green rabbit population and save birds from feral cats. The plan worked well, but then the bobkitten population itself grew out of hand.

As he walks, Snowman also hears celebratory sounds from a Craker mating ceremony, in which four men have sex with a single woman. Crake engineered the Crakers to mate only once every three years, in a ritual designed to eliminate sexual competition. Snowman's mind slips back to the time he visited Crake at the Watson-Crick Institute when Crake spoke about "how much needless despair has been caused by a series of biological mismatches." Jimmy tried to convince Crake that eliminating sexual competition would also eliminate courtship behavior, which in turn provides the source of much art. Crake, however, simply concluded that art is little more than "a stab at getting laid."

Snowman rests against a tree, feeling dejected.

ANALYSIS

Chapter 7 introduces more information about the genetic makeup of the Crakers, which further suggests just how much thought and care Crake put into his creations. More than simply representing the culmination of Crake's research and his brilliance as a biologist, the genetic complexity of the Crakers demonstrates that Crake designed his new race knowing they would need to survive harsh, postapocalyptic conditions. With this in mind, he gave the men the ability to repel predators via the scent in their urine, he endowed adults with the ability to purr at a healing frequency, and he altered both male and female hormone rhythms so they would only mate once every three years. All these genetic modifications, along with the others already indicated in previous chapters, would enable the Crakers to survive in the wild, even after civilization's collapse. The fact that Crake imbued his new humans with all of these abilities implies both that he knew some kind of apocalyptic event would bring an end to civilization and that he intended his creations to represent a new start for humanity.

Crake's genetic designs aimed to develop new behavioral patterns that would in turn correct problems that have long plagued human societies. Most crucially, Crake changed the manner and frequency of how humans mate in an attempt to eliminate all forms of sexual competition. Eliminating sexual competition would provide two main benefits. First, it would ensure that no energy gets wasted in trying to find a mate. And second, it would prevent aggression, particularly amongst males. The revised frequency of mating provided another important though less obvious benefit. Since female Crakers only mate once every three years, the Craker tribe as a whole reproduces at a steady rate that replaces the current population without adding significantly to their overall numbers. And without a rapidly expanding population, there would also be no need to dramatically expand the size of their territory. Crake's therefore aimed for his new breed of human to avoid the kind of overpopulation that had previously overburdened the planet and exhausted its limited natural resources.

The conversation between Crake and Jimmy that appears at the end of the chapter introduces a new theme about the fundamental difference between Crake as a "numbers guy" and Jimmy as a "word guy." When Crake first told Jimmy his theory about sexual competition and the "needless despair" it causes, Jimmy saw that

Crake's perspective posed a threat not just to his own sexuality but also to his interest in art. Whereas Crake hadn't shown much interest in sex, Jimmy had felt drawn to women and curious about sex since his high school days. Crake may not have seen why anyone would want to spend their energy on courtship, but that was precisely what Jimmy focused much of his own energy on. But in addition to threatening the pleasure of courtship behavior, Jimmy recognized that Crake's theory also posed a threat to art. Reasoning that much art begins from thwarted desire, Jimmy concluded that eliminating sexual competition would also eliminate the need for art. That is, if no one knew what it felt like to be a spurned lover, then no one would be able to connect with the basic emotional message that drives artistic creation.

CHAPTER 8

SUMMARY

> *Nature is to zoos as God is to churches.*
> *(See* QUOTATIONS, *p. 64)*

The narrative returns to when Jimmy and Crake graduated from HelthWyzer High and various universities participated in a Student Auction to bid on pupils they wanted to recruit. Whereas the prestigious Watson-Crick won Crake for a high price, the less prestigious Martha Graham Academy claimed Jimmy in a half-hearted bidding war. Jimmy's father greeted the news with lukewarm praise. Ramona, who had since officially become Jimmy's stepmother, was more exuberant with her approval. Even so, Jimmy hated her "new matronly air."

Crake's mother had died a month before Crake and Jimmy's graduation. The circumstances of her death remained unclear, but somehow she'd come into contact with a dangerous "bioform" that quickly infected and killed her by dissolving her flesh. Crake had to watch her die, and, much to Jimmy's dismay, Crake recounted the experience with more curiosity than horror.

In the summer after Jimmy and Crake graduated from high school, global tensions escalated over a genetically modified coffee bush produced by the Happicuppa coffee company. The new type of bush threatened to put small local farms out of business and consolidate the global coffee industry into a monopoly. One night, while watching the news, Jimmy spotted a glimpse of his mother in a crowd of activists protesting Happicuppa.

Crake noticed her too, and he tried to connect with Jimmy by recounting the story of how his father "buggered off" and fell off a pleebland overpass during rush hour. In contrast to the general opinion that he committed suicide, Crake remained suspicious about the circumstances of the event. In the present time Snowman scolds himself for having missed the underlying message of Crake's story.

Jimmy began his studies at Martha Graham Academy, a fading school for the arts and humanities that he found disappointing. Although Jimmy thought it was "pleasant to contemplate" the arts and humanities, he recognized that they were "no longer central to anything." He enrolled in a program called Problematics, which he believed would lead to a career in advertising.

At first Jimmy shared a dorm suite with a fundamentalist vegan named Bernice, who terrorized him for both his eating habits and his sexual activity. He complained to Student Services and moved to a new room, where he felt freer to pursue relationships with women.

At the holidays, Jimmy visited Crake at Watson-Crick, which had a much more impressive and well-maintained campus than Martha Graham. Jimmy noticed some unusually large butterflies fluttering around, and he wanted to know if the butterflies were real or if they were also created by students. Crake responded by challenging Jimmy's distinction between "real" and "fake."

During the tour of Watson-Crick, Crake introduced Jimmy to numerous ongoing research-and-development projects. One such project was located in the BioDefences lab, which housed a series of cages containing friendly-looking dogs. Crake warned Jimmy not to approach the cages. These animals, called "wolvogs," had been bred to look like ordinary dogs, but they were extremely dangerous. Jimmy again expressed concern about the development of such unnatural creatures, and Crake responded by rejecting the idea of "Nature" with a "capital N."

On the second to last evening of the visit, Crake told Jimmy that HelthWyzer had been developing new diseases and distributing them to the population through their vitamin pills. Crake's father found out and wanted to blow the whistle. He told his wife and supervisor, and one of them must have reported him, because HelthWyzer had him executed.

On their last evening together, Crake told Jimmy that he had become a Grandmaster on Extinctathon. He also explained that MaddAddam, the figure who monitored the game, was not a person but rather a group of people who were involved in a variety of incidents of bioterrorism. Jimmy warned Crake how dangerous it could be to get involved, but Crake shrugged off Jimmy's concern and said he was just curious.

ANALYSIS

As Crake and Jimmy part ways for college, the narrative begins to stage a symbolic conflict between the sciences and the arts. This symbolic conflict comes into focus through the significant differences separating the institutions each young man attended. Crake went to an elite and well-funded science academy with energetic and engaged students and faculty. Students there had ample opportunities to work on top-level, state-of-the-art research for government as well as private contracts. Jimmy, by contrast, attended a poorly funded arts and humanities academy where everything—including the faculty, students, campus, and security—seemed lackluster and disengaged. The differences between Watson-Crick Institute and Martha Graham Academy reflect a social and cultural hierarchy that systematically privileges the sciences over the arts. In a world so completely dominated by the sciences, Jimmy, whose gifts and talents tended toward the arts, felt devalued and struggled to see what he had to offer. Jimmy's choice to major in Problematics so that he could pursue a career in advertising demonstrates his belief that the only way to make himself valuable would be to exploit his talents in the service of profitable science and tech industries.

Unlike Crake, who was too busy for romantic relationships, Jimmy had a lot of time to explore intimacy, and his various relationships with women introduce some troubling patterns. Jimmy had a melancholic personality that attracted women who wanted to tend his emotional wounds. Jimmy imagined these women found a sense of purpose in working on him, and he amplified his melancholy demeanor to keep them interested. The story of his mother made an especially strong impression. Though Jimmy employed emotionally manipulative behavior in his relationships with women, he also believed that he loved them. Jimmy's emotional confusion about his love for these women echoes the emotional confusion related to his feelings about his mother. Recall that when he was a young boy, Jimmy strongly desired to alleviate his mother's sadness, and he considered this desire a form of love. In his college years, when Jimmy sought women to tend his emotional wounds, he symbolically took the place of his own mother as the wounded love object.

The account of Jimmy's visit to Watson-Crick introduces additional thematic material related to genetic engineering, this time specifically related to the blurry distinction between what is natural versus unnatural, "real" versus "fake." When Jimmy saw massive butterflies flapping around the Watson-Crick campus, he suspected that they were created in a lab and assumed that this meant that they were in some way fake. For Crake, however, the distinction between "real" and "fake" is false. Despite being created by humans, these butterflies actually existed in the material world. They lived, died, and bred, just like every other species and hence must be considered real. The issue of distinguishing between real and fake returned near the end of the visit, when Jimmy expressed his feeling that the wolvogs were unnatural, since they reversed the centuries of breeding that had transformed wild wolves into domesticated dogs. Here, too, Crake dismissed Jimmy's language of natural versus unnatural. Crake implied that the very concept of "Nature" (with a capital N) is bogus. He implied that genetic engineering represents a natural activity because it was developed by humans, who are themselves a part of nature.

Crake's hypothesis about HelthWyzer, which he explained to Jimmy on the second-to-last night of their visit, introduces an important theme related to the immorality of corporate power. According to Crake, HelthWyzer had a fundamentally contradictory business model. On the one hand, the company sought to cure ill people and eliminate disease. And yet, if the company really achieved its aim and eliminated all diseases, then there would be no way for the company to make money. Thus, to ensure its own profitability, the company had to invent its own diseases and distribute them among the public at large. Crake's hypothesis brings to light the contradictory logic of corporate power, which subdues the very people it relies on for revenue. Whereas Crake's father sought to expose the immorality of corporate power, Crake himself would later capitalize on this logic to advance his own agenda, as later chapters in the novel demonstrate.

CHAPTER 9

SUMMARY

Snowman continues on his way to the RejoovenEsense Compound. He moves through a former residential sector that is now slowly being reclaimed by vines and other natural growth. As he proceeds, Snowman wonders about whether others have survived. He also thinks about what the survivors' descendants will make of the ruins of civilization. Vultures circle overhead, and as noon approaches, Snowman worries about finding shelter.

Snowman arrives at the twelve-foot-high wall that surrounds RejoovenEsense and passes through the outer gate, which is no longer electrified. He makes note of a trail of objects that people left behind when they fled the Compound. After passing the gate and the abandoned security checkpoint, Snowman proceeds down the main street toward the residences. He goes into a medium-sized house, where he finds a small amount of bourbon in the liquor cabinet and a dead man in the bathroom. He finds the corpse of a woman in the bedroom, and her pixie haircut reminds him of a wig Oryx used to have. Snowman also walks through a child's room, but the child's body isn't in there.

Snowman proceeds to the kitchen hoping to find food, but someone else has already raided the cupboards, leaving nothing more than stale cereal, three packets of cashews, and a tin of SoyOBoy sardines. He also finds a working flashlight, candle ends, and matches, and then stuffs everything into a garbage bag. Next Snowman goes down the hall to the home office, where he finds a computer as well as a pile of reference books. Snowman hypothesizes that the dead man in the bathroom must have worked as an advertiser or speechwriter for RejoovenEsense, and then imagines that he's broken into his own childhood home.

Snowman leaves, hoping to find another house with a stash of canned goods. But as soon as he crawls out a window he's confronted by a group of pigoons. He stands still until the pigoons wander off, then cautiously move away, thinking he could take refuge in the nearby checkpoint gatehouse. At the same time ominous clouds roll in, signaling a coming tornado.

Rain, wind, and thunder swell, and Snowman ducks into a gatehouse. Inside he finds two dead men in biosuits and a mess of scattered paper. The storm outside frightens Snowman, and his hands shake. He worries about the possibility that there are rats in the gate-house, and that if water floods in, they will swarm around him. As he curls his legs up on the chair, a voice in his head counsels, "Having to face a crisis causes you to grow as a person."

In the dark he lights a match, eats a packet of cashews, and drinks the partial bottle of bourbon. He hears a woman's voice, possibly Oryx's, assure him, "You're doing really well." A puff of air blows out Snowman's candle, leaving him in the dark once again.

ANALYSIS

Chapter 9 provides the reader with more fragments of insight into the nature of the apocalyptic event that led to Snowman's pres-ent. In particular, the details in this chapter indicate that the event happened suddenly and caused a sense of panic among the inhabit-ants of the RejoovenEsense Compound. The reader knows that people must have picked up and left without much planning, both because of the trail of belongings that leads from the residences and out of the Compound, and because of Snowman's conviction that the houses in RejooveEsense will likely still be full of supplies. Furthermore, the fact that people clearly fled the RejoovenEsense Compound suggests that Snowman may be entering ground zero—that is, the epicenter of the apocalyptic event. Although the full details of the event will not appear until later chapters, the current chapter uses foreshadowing to build a sense of suspense for the reader.

At the same time as Chapter 9 offers fragmentary suggestions about the past, it also shows Snowman thinking about the bleakness of the future. The chapter opens with Snowman wondering about what future generations might think when they examine the ruins of the former civilization. Although Snowman doesn't make any specific conclusions about what these fictional people will think, his thoughts nevertheless suggest a bleak future. For one thing, as he wanders, he observes plant life already overtaking residential areas. This image of nature reclaiming the ruins of civilization echoes simi-lar images from earlier in the novel, as when Snowman made note of some overgrown rooftop gardens in Chapter 5. In addition to this speculation about nature's reclamation of civilization, Snowman also recalls a point that Crake once made about how the elimination of a single generation of humans would bring an end to civilization. Even if there were survivors, there would be no effective way for them to resurrect the vast amount of complex knowledge that would have been lost. Snowman may not explicitly think about how bad the future will be, but his observations and recollections throughout the chapter nonetheless suggest a bleak outlook.

As Snowman arrives at the RejoovenEsense Compound, alone and imagining the panic of all those who once lived there, the narrative revisits the theme of Snowman's loneliness. A strong sense of loneliness flares up both in the house where he searches for supplies and in the gatehouse where he takes shelter from the tornado. While searching the house, Snowman has an uncanny feeling that he's in his own childhood home and that he is the child who was missing from the kid's bedroom he found upstairs. This uncanny sensation partly relates to the fact that the apocalyptic event made Snowman an orphan, and it surfaces just after he finds an office with a stack of reference books, which make him speculate that the dead man upstairs worked in advertising. As the next chapter will make clear, Jimmy went on to have a career in advertising after graduating from Martha Graham Academy. Thus, in addition to seeing himself as the absent child, Snowman also envisions the dead man he found upstairs as a representation of a former self (i.e., Jimmy) that perished in the apocalypse.

CHAPTER 10

SUMMARY

> He knew he was faltering, trying to keep his footing.
> Everything in his life was temporary, ungrounded.
> Language itself had lost its solidity; it had become
> thin, contingent, slippery, a viscid film on which he was
> sliding around like an eyeball on a plate.
>
> *(See* QUOTATIONS, *p. 65)*

Jimmy graduated from Martha Graham and began working for the Academy's library. The job entailed sorting through old books, selecting some to be digitized and others to be destroyed. Jimmy, however, could not bear to throw away any books, so he lost his job partway into the summer.

After losing his job, he moved in with his then-girlfriend, Amanda Payne. Amanda was a conceptual artist who had been working on a series of Vulture Sculptures, which involved transporting truckloads of dead animal parts to fields or parking lots, arranging the parts into words, and photographing the action once vultures descended. She only used four-letter words for her installations, like "WHOM" and "GUTS," and she claimed that "vulturizing" these words activated them and brought them to life.

Amanda had two roommates, who frequently shared their opinions on the state of the world. For instance, they claimed that humankind was doomed from the time when agriculture was invented. Jimmy did not get along with Amanda's roommates, and he rejected their theory of humanity.

Eventually Jimmy landed an advertising job at AnooYoo, a company that designed and sold a variety of self-help products. Jimmy got the job due to his undergraduate dissertation on twentieth-century self-help books. At AnooYoo, Jimmy quickly mastered the art of using fear, desire, and revulsion in his advertising campaigns, which made him a hit with his bosses. Jimmy got a promotion, and he also began to sleep with a variety of women whom he thought of as his "lovers." Many of these women were married, and none of them wanted to leave their husbands for Jimmy.

Jimmy's life at AnooYoo grew increasingly tiresome and depressing over the years. Crake, by contrast, already had an impressive career. Soon after graduating early from Watson-Crick, he began working at RejoovenEsense. He quickly climbed the ladder there and became the head of his own "white-hot" special project.

Around this time, Crake told Jimmy that Uncle Pete had died from a virus that took him down suddenly and violently. Jimmy asked whether Crake was there when Uncle Pete died, and Crake responded: "In a manner of speaking." After this news, communication between Jimmy and Crake dwindled.

As time passed, Jimmy felt more and more restless. Sex no longer gave him the same thrill, and the news was full of stories about plagues, famines, floods, and droughts. The news also reported on a story about adolescent girls who had been brought from other countries and locked in garages. Jimmy thought he recognized one of the girls, and he wondered if she was the same girl he and Crake had seen in the HottTotts video years prior.

In his fifth year at AnooYoo, agents from the CorpSeCorps appeared at Jimmy's apartment and showed him a video of a blindfolded woman about to be executed. A Corpsman in the video removed the woman's blindfold, and it was Jimmy's mother. She looked straight into the camera and said, "Goodbye. Remember Killer. I love you. Don't let me down." The camera then panned back out, and the soldiers completed the execution. The Corpsmen wanted to know what she meant by "Killer," and Jimmy informed them that Killer was the name of his pet rakunk.

In the weeks following the Corpsmen's visit, Jimmy spiraled into depression. He retreated from communication and began to drink alone at night. Language no longer felt solid, and he no longer took comfort in words.

ANALYSIS

Jimmy's relationship with Amanda marked a significant transformation in how he related to women. Amanda had endured a number of traumatizing experiences in her life, having grown up in a working-class family that the narrator describes as "abusive, white-trash, and sugar-overdosed." Jimmy found Amanda's emotional wounds compelling, and he wanted to "mend" her. During his earlier college years, Jimmy had exaggerated his melancholy personality to bait women who might want to fix him. With Amanda, Jimmy has a similar desire but in reverse. Whereas before he positioned himself as the love object that others pursued, now he positioned himself as the one who pursues the love object. This new pattern reappeared later, in his fascination with the girl imprisoned in the garage. Jimmy's interest in this girl stemmed from his desire to mend her psychological wounds. This change in Jimmy's romantic behavior also marked a shift in his sexuality, which, as the rest of the chapter indicates, became increasingly obsessive, to the point of addiction.

Although Jimmy disliked Amanda's housemates and dismissed their theory that humanity was doomed from the start, the reader, who knows about the apocalypse to come, is more likely to find their bleak theory credible. Though the narrator doesn't fully spell out the logic of the housemates' theory, the implication is that the seeds of the world's current environmental crises were sewn back when humans first invented agriculture some six or seven thousand years ago. Before that, humans had survived by foraging and hunting. Agriculture stabilized the food supply, making it possible for the human population to expand. Over thousands of years, this expansion eventually led to a population so large that people felt the need to fight over territory. Hence the housemates' conclusion that ever since the invention of agriculture, human society had proved itself "a sort of monster, its main by-products being corpses and rubble." At the time, Jimmy dismissed this theory of humanity as absurd. However, the news stories he encountered later about climate change and related environmental disasters suggested that Amanda's housemates may have been right about how humans had doomed themselves.

Crake's news about his Uncle Pete's death struck Jimmy as suspicious, particularly given how the mysterious circumstances of his death echoed the mysterious circumstances of Crake's mother's death many years prior when she was suddenly infected by a violent, unknown virus. Crake witnessed her death, and when he recounted the experience to Jimmy, he spoke with curiosity rather than horror. At the time, Crake's emotional distance alarmed Jimmy, and a similar feeling arose when Crake informed Jimmy of Uncle Pete's death. Just like Crake's mother, Uncle Pete died suddenly from a virus that didn't infect anyone else. Jimmy wanted to know whether Crake had been present to witness the death, as he had been with his mother, and Crake responded cryptically: "In a manner of speaking." As Jimmy would come to suspect much later, Crake had something to do with Uncle Pete's death. From Snowman's retrospective perspective, this moment represents one of many signs of Crake's sociopathic personality that went unnoticed at the time, but which led directly to the apocalypse to come.

The most significant event in Chapter 10 comes near the end, when Jimmy learned of his mother's execution. By this point, many years had passed since his mother had abandoned him. Over those years, Jimmy continued to feel the pain of his mother's absence as well as anger and resentment. Yet these feelings about his mother also grew increasingly dull over those same years due to the CorpSeCorp's frequent appearances in his life to interrogate him about his mother's whereabouts. When the Corpsmen showed up for yet another interrogation, Jimmy had become so used to the sessions that he wasn't prepared for the footage the agents showed him of his mother's execution. Furthermore, the words she uttered when she turned to the camera were clearly meant for Jimmy, and they immediately brought back a flood of competing emotions. The word "goodbye" offered him a kind of closure he never had after she left him, but at the same time the words "I love you" also reactivated Jimmy's longing for her. These are words he didn't hear much as a boy, and the belated news of his mother's love sent Jimmy into a spiraling depression.

SUMMARY & ANALYSIS

Chapter 11

Summary

Snowman has a dream of himself as a child waiting for his mother to come. Snowman wakes up in the gatehouse, but he can't tell how much time has passed since he fell asleep. He hears a scraping sound coming from a hole in the corner where a large crab is scrounging in the rubble.

Snowman sets out from the gatehouse, but three blocks away he comes upon the pigoons from the previous day. Snowman hurries back to the gatehouse, and, knowing the pigoons will be able to nose their way in, he retreats into another room where he finds a door leading to a stairwell. He scrambles up the stairs just as the pigoons force their way into the gatehouse. The pigoons can't follow him up the stairs.

Upstairs Snowman finds himself in one of the two watchtowers that flank the gatehouse. There are no bodies up there, which makes Snowman suspect that the guards fled the premises like everyone else, attempting to avoid the contagion. He suspects that the men in the biosuits downstairs may have been the guards.

Snowman finds a variety of supplies in the watchtower, including a pack of cigarettes, some food, and two bottles of beer. He also finds a windup radio. He searches the AM and FM bands but hears nothing. He switches to the short-wave radio and hears a voice speaking in Russian. He switches again to the CB radio to see if he can find a local transmission. He turns the radio dial to the receive function, and the voice of a man asking "Anyone out there?" comes in faintly. Snowman tries to respond, and though he has second thoughts about his haste to reply, he nevertheless feels elated by the idea of other survivors like himself.

Snowman notices a cut on his foot and tries to clean the wound with expired antibiotic ointment. Afterwards, he lies down on a cot. He thinks about how a dead man used sleep there and how that man couldn't have known what was coming. By contrast, Snowman thinks, Jimmy did have clues but failed to read the signs. Even so, Snowman wonders whether it would have made any difference if he had killed Crake sooner.

The next day he eats, packs a laundry bag with supplies, and escapes from the watchtower onto the twelve-foot-high rampart wall surrounding the Compound. He hurries along the rampart wall toward his next destination, the domed structure known as Paradice. Along the way Snowman notices a trail of smoke in the distance. Snowman considers that the smoke might come from a fire started by lightning, or else by the Crakers, but he remains suspicious of either explanation. He eats a Joltbar and continues on his way.

ANALYSIS

Chapter 11 features a lot of foreshadowing related to events from Snowman's past that the narrative has not yet fully explained. For one thing, the reader gets more details about the nature of the apocalyptic event. Snowman specifically thinks that the watchtower guards may have tried to flee the facility in biosuits because they wanted to avoid a contagion, suggesting that whatever caused the apocalyptic event may have been connected to an epidemic. For another thing, the reader learns that the apocalyptic event wasn't simply local. In addition to Snowman's discovery of a Russian-language message coming from far away via the short-wave radio, he also wonders whether people in places like New Zealand and Madagascar escaped. These thoughts clearly indicate the global reach of the apocalyptic event. But the most significant piece of fore-shadowing in this chapter comes in the revelation that Snowman killed Crake. This revelation creates a feeling of suspense for the rest of the novel.

As Snowman recalls the story of his relationship with Crake and laments that he failed to see the signs that were right in front of him, the reader learns that Snowman feels some degree of responsibility and guilt for the apocalyptic event. This revelation of Snowman's guilt points the reader both forward and backward in the narrative since it makes the reader curious about the extent of Snowman's responsibility and rehink what is already known about Snowman. Up until this point, the novel has presented Snowman as a victim. Though predisposed to cynicism, and despite his questionable treatment of women, Snowman comes across as an essentially good person. He's a long-suffering casualty of his friend's ambitions, and despite the hopelessness of the situation created by Crake, he continues to look out for the Crakers. But if Snowman was personally involved in the events that led to the apocalypse, then that revelation makes the reader question his motivations and his apparent innocence.

For all that this chapter focuses on the catastrophic event that lies in Snowman's past, the multiple signs of other survivors give Snowman his first sense of hope for the future. At the beginning of Chapter 9, Snowman speculated vaguely about a bleak future in which nature would overtake the ruins of civilization. In this chapter, however, the radio messages and smoke signals provide Snowman with two important signs that he is not as alone in the world as he previously believed. These signs also provide Snowman with the only surge of joy and hope that he has felt thus far in the novel. Yet Snowman is deeply conditioned by his cynicism. After he tries to respond to one of the radio messages he immediately regrets having done so, and his suspicious reaction shows that he struggles to believe that the future could really turn out okay.

CHAPTER 12 (PLEEBCRAWL–PARADICE)

SUMMARY

> "Immortality," said Crake, "is a concept. If you take 'mortality' as being, not death, but the foreknowlege of it and the fear of it, then 'immortality' is the absence of such fear. Babies are immortal. Edit out the fear and you'll be . . ."
> "Sounds like Applied Rhetoric 101," said Jimmy.
> "What?"
> "Never mind. Martha Graham stuff."
> (See QUOTATIONS, p. 65)

Snowman walks along the rampart wall and wonders what Crake needed him for.

The narrative then shifts back in time to Jimmy, who had been feeling depressed and avoiding human contact. One morning, Crake showed up at Jimmy's building to check in on him after learning about his mother's death. Crake took Jimmy for a weekend in the pleeblands, and before they left, he gave Jimmy a vaccine to protect him from any diseases he might encounter there. While they were out, Crake offered Jimmy a job at RejoovenEsense, and Jimmy agreed.

When Jimmy returned to AnooYoo the following week, his coworkers already knew about his new job at RejoovenEsense. Crake had already informed everyone who needed to know, and he had also made arrangements for Jimmy's travel and for his apartment to get packed up and transported to the new Compound.

Upon Jimmy's arrival, Crake gave him a tour of RejoovenEsense. Jimmy found the new Compound even more impressive than

Watson-Crick. When Jimmy asked Crake what paid for everything, Crake responded: "Grief in the face of inevitable death."

Over lunch, Crake explained to Jimmy that he and his colleagues did research on immortality. Crake further explained that his unit was working on two main initiatives, the first of which was a pill called BlyssPluss. The pill had four functions. First, it protected against all sexually transmitted diseases. Second, it provided an unlimited libido. Third, it prolonged youth. And fourth, it sterilized the user so that they would no longer be capable of producing children. The fourth function was not to be marketed publicly. After discussing some of the moral and financial implications of the new drug, Crake informed Jimmy that his job would be to run the BlyssPluss ad campaign.

After lunch, Crake gave Jimmy a tour of Paradice, the heavily secured facility to which only Crake and his team had access. Each of the employees inside the facility wore a name tag with the name of an extinct animal, and Crake explained that every person working at Paradice was a Grandmaster in the game Extinctathon—that is, they were, collectively, MaddAddam. Crake had tracked each one down and persuaded them that they would be safer working for him than on their own.

Inside the Paradice facility, Crake revealed the second major project he and his team were working on. He led Jimmy to a two-way mirror that looked in on a large, enclosed space with plants, trees, and a domed bubble "sky." Inside the enclosure, Jimmy saw a group of perfectly formed naked people: the Children of Crake.

Later that evening, Crake explained how he had been working on these genetically enhanced humans for the past seven years. Crake had programmed them to die suddenly at the age of thirty. He reasoned that if he could take away the foreknowledge and fear of death, the result would be a kind of immortality. Crake also explained that the individuals in the enclosure were "floor models" with an extensive range of genetically optimized characteristics, and that part of his plan was to make each of these characteristics available to parents who wanted genetic enhancements for their children.

ANALYSIS

In the first half of Chapter 12, Crake comes to look more and more like a kind of savior. First, the reader learns that he saved Jimmy from his spiraling depression and his dead-end job at AnooYoo. In doing this, Crake reprises the role he played when he and Jimmy were boys. Just as his friendship helped Jimmy through the difficult period after his mother ran away, so too did his sudden appearance at Jimmy's door save him from despair following the news of his mother's execution. Later on in the chapter, the reader learns that Crake had also used the significant resources available to him to track down all of the other Extinctathon Grandmasters and convince them to work for him at Paradice. Here again Crake acts like a savior since all of those people were in trouble with the authorities for their years of involvement in bioterrorism.

Crake's savior-like appearance has an important link to the symbolism of his Paradice facility. Though spelled differently, as if to suggest a game of chance played with a pair of dice, "Paradice" references the biblical Paradise, where God placed the first humans, Adam and Eve. As the head authority in control of the Paradice facility, Crake symbolically positioned himself not just as a savior but as a God figure. However, the full extent of Crake's God complex only becomes clear in the context of the two-phase plan he developed. The first phase involved the distribution of the BlyssPluss pill to put a stop to human reproduction. The second phase involved introducing a new breed of genetically enhanced humans that could replace the existing human population, which at that point would have stopped growing. In other words, Crake has, like God, created his own version of Paradise, populated with representatives of a new and improved human race.

This chapter also shows the extreme extent to which Crake has pushed his earlier theory about sexual competition. Recall that in Chapter 7, Crake explained to Jimmy his theory that sexual competition represented both a waste of energy and the primary source of aggression among humans. BlyssPluss represents Crake's response to the problem of sexual competition. If he could keep the general population feeling young, enjoying a healthy libido, and safe from sexually transmitted diseases, then, theoretically, everyone would have a happy sex life without the need for aggressive, competitive behavior. That said, Crake clearly did not believe in the ability of BlyssPluss to achieve his goal on its own since the pill also covertly sterilized its user, thereby preventing reproduction. Crake's desire to revise human courtship behavior while simultaneously putting an end to human reproduction demonstrates an extreme moral impertinence that is in line with his sociopathic personality traits, which have appeared throughout the novel.

A deep irony persists in all of Crake's theories, an irony that Crake himself didn't appear to notice, and which Snowman only recognized with regard to how Crake, the staunch atheist, played God. Thus far, the novel has staged a competition between the sciences and the humanities, a competition channeled through the relationship between Crake and Jimmy. Whereas Crake and his rise to power demonstrate the high value placed on scientific research, Jimmy's mediocre advertising career shows the relatively poor value society places on humanities-based skills. And yet, this chapter shows that for all that Crake abides by scientific rationalism, the details of his experiments have all hinged not on scientific principles but on philosophical perspectives of human society and the human condition. Consider Crake's theory of immortality. For him, achieving immortality was not primarily a scientific goal. He made this clear when he indicated that other scientists were close to discovering how to prolong life indefinitely. By contrast, Crake took a fundamentally philosophical approach to immortality in which it wasn't death that needed to be banished but the fear of death. Considering Crake's identification with the sciences, his philosophical solution to the question of immortality is deeply ironic.

CHAPTER 12 (CRAKE IN LOVE–AIRLOCK)

SUMMARY

A few days after he arrived at Paradice, Jimmy noticed a woman inside the bubble dome and instantly recognized her. Crake told Jimmy that her name was Oryx and that her job was to teach the people in the enclosure. She also traveled frequently, distributing trial samples of BlyssPluss in "sex clinics" around the world. Jimmy quickly realized that Crake was in love with her. When Jimmy asked Crake where he found her, Crake replied that he had met her when he was a student at Watson-Crick. She was a prostitute.

Jimmy felt tormented by desire for Oryx, but out of respect for Crake he didn't make any moves. Eventually, though, Oryx came to Jimmy and seduced him.

One night, Jimmy asked Oryx about her experience in the garage. At first, Oryx insisted that she was never kept in a garage, but when Jimmy pressed her, she said that the man who locked her up was kind. In spite of her admission, Jimmy suspected that Oryx might merely have humored him.

In the present time, Snowman thinks about a scene with Oryx that he's replayed many times, and he wonders to himself what he could have done differently. He remembers a night when Oryx wanted to go get takeout, and she promised she'd come right back with pizza. Jimmy tried to stall her and fantasized out loud about running away together.

Snowman recalls bad omens that he missed at the time, such as when Crake asked him if he would kill someone he loved to spare them pain. At another time, Crake informed Jimmy that if anything happened to him, Jimmy would have to look after the Paradice Project. When Jimmy asked if it would be better to put Oryx in charge, Crake responded that if he wasn't around, then Oryx wouldn't be around either.

Returning to the scene before Oryx left for takeout, Jimmy voiced his suspicion that Crake knew about their relationship, but Oryx dismissed Jimmy's worry that Crake felt jealous. Before she left, she asked Jimmy to take care of the Crakers if she and Crake disappeared.

Jimmy waited for Oryx for a long time. News reports about simultaneous incidents of bioterrorism started coming in from around the world, and since Crake was off premises, the staff called Jimmy to Paradice headquarters. Jimmy's phone rang and Oryx was on the line. Crying, she explained that the BlyssPluss pills she had been disbursing had caused a plague. She apologized to Jimmy and swore that she didn't know. Then the connection broke.

Later that night, Crake called and assured Jimmy that everything was under control. He said he was at the pizza place in the mall and that he would come to Paradice shortly. Jimmy changed the door code, and he picked up a spraygun from the emergency storeroom.

When Crake arrived, he couldn't get into the facility. Jimmy explained that he was following Crake's instructions not to let anyone in. Crake assured Jimmy that both he and Jimmy were immune since he'd hidden the antibody serum in the vaccine they'd taken before going to the pleeblands. Jimmy opened the door. Crake entered the room. He held a knife in one hand, and his other arm was wrapped around Oryx. Crake dropped Oryx over his arm, told Jimmy "I'm counting on you," and slit her throat. Then Jimmy shot Crake.

ANALYSIS

The second half of Chapter 12 at last reveals how Jimmy and Oryx met and how their romantic relationship developed in the shadow of Crake's love for Oryx. Oryx's appearance at the Paradice facility was foreshadowed in Chapter 8 when Crake navigated to a secret Extinctathon game room using the image of Oryx from the HottTotts website as his virtual passkey. Jimmy had felt profoundly affected by that image and kept a physical copy with him throughout the years, but up to that point, Jimmy had no idea that Crake felt similarly intrigued by the image. This background helps explain how, at Paradice, Jimmy could recognize Crake's love for Oryx so quickly. The fact that both Crake and Jimmy had felt an affection for Oryx for so long also points to her symbolic importance as a shared object of desire and hence a threat to their friendship. When Oryx took both Crake and Jimmy as lovers, she activated the implicit sense of rivalry that had long persisted between the two men. In other words, Oryx's appearance at Paradice and her initiation of a love triangle with Crake and Jimmy ultimately heralded the end of the two men's friendship.

From a psychological perspective, Jimmy's relationship with Oryx was an extension of his previous relationships with women and particularly his relationship with Amanda Payne. Just as he wanted to mend Amanda's traumas, Jimmy obsessed over Oryx and her life story. However, Jimmy's interest in Oryx's past quickly grew invasive, as when he interrogated her about her experience being locked in a garage. Although Jimmy's interest in Oryx followed a similar, if exaggerated, psychological pattern that he had established with Amanda, Oryx herself was a very different person from Amanda. Specifically, she didn't find Jimmy's concern romantic, and at every turn, she deflected his questions and rejected his assumptions about how her experiences had affected her. Whereas Jimmy approached Oryx like a broken person who needed someone to put her back together, Oryx insisted on her own integrity and wholeness. It is only in the present time that Snowman can retrospectively see that Oryx was probably only humoring him when she admitted to any feelings of trauma at all.

The second half of Chapter 12 recounts how the first hours of the plague and the final hours of Oryx's and Crake's lives passed in a jumble that left Jimmy confused about what Crake's plan had actually been. It's clear that Crake had laced his BlyssPluss pills with a contagion that had a delayed release and which he designed to cause a virulent plague that would kill a significant portion of the world's population. What's less clear, though, is what Crake himself had planned to do following the plague's outbreak. Prior to the outbreak, he instructed Jimmy to take charge of Paradice should something happen and Crake not be around. Later on, Oryx said something almost identical, suggesting that Crake must have let her in on his plan. Yet Oryx also denied knowing about the BlyssPluss pills when she called Jimmy to tell him what had happened. Ultimately, Crake and Oryx both died before Jimmy could get any answers, leaving him suspended in ambiguity. This ambiguity is important, since it shows the reader another source of the tortured psyche Snowman has exhibited since the beginning of the novel. Snowman doesn't have all the details about what happened and why, and this not knowing continues to haunt him.

CHAPTER 13

SUMMARY

After the storm, and with an increasingly painful foot, Snowman progresses along the rampart wall toward Paradice. He reaches the watchtower nearest the facility and uses his sheet as a rope to rappel down the wall. Once on the ground, he proceeds to Paradice. He passes through the airlock and finds the remains of Oryx and Crake. Snowman locates the medical supplies and gives himself a shot of antibiotics. The following morning, Snowman's foot feels better.

Snowman recalls what happened after he shot Crake. He sealed the inner door, leaving Oryx and Crake in the airlock, then got drunk on Scotch and fell asleep. He woke up to other Paradice staff trying to get in, but Jimmy ignored them. Later in the day an angry CorpSeCorps agent working for RejoovenEsense called Jimmy. Jimmy convinced the agent not to raid the Paradice facility, claiming that it was contaminated. He also implied that Crake had sold his research to a rival company and run away to Bermuda.

After the outbreak, Jimmy checked on the Crakers three times a day. He spent the rest of his time eating, sleeping, and watching news reports about the pandemic. Newscasters discussed conspiracy theories about the origin of the contagion and reported the gradual breakdown of transportation and communications systems.

Jimmy thought a lot about why Crake had done what he did, but he couldn't come to any definite conclusions. One theory was that Crake had staged a suicide, killing Oryx with the expectation that Jimmy would kill him in turn. But Jimmy didn't understand why Crake would have wanted to die. Was he afraid that CorpSeCorps agents would torture him and he'd give up the antidote? Or was he just wracked with jealousy? Jimmy had no way of knowing.

Eventually Jimmy realized he couldn't stay in Paradice much longer. The Crakers were running out of plants to eat, and he needed to get them someplace where they would be safe.

In the present, Snowman finds a letter than he wrote before he escorted the Crakers from Paradice. The letter details everything Jimmy knew about what had happened and how Crake was to blame but then cuts off in the middle of a sentence speculating on Crake's motives. Snowman can't remember what his own speculations had been at the time.

Jimmy went into the enclosure to meet the Crakers, where he introduced himself as "Snowman." He informed the Crakers that Oryx had gone away and that Crake had sent him in her stead. Jimmy also explained that Oryx and Crake wanted them to go to a better place where there would be more food. The Crakers asked Snowman about his clothes and his facial hair, and he skillfully made up stories about both. He enjoyed his own ability to dance "gracefully around the truth."

Snowman planned a route out of Paradice, through the Compound, and toward the ocean. Along the way the group encountered several desperate people who were clearly infected. Snowman shot each one with a spraygun, and he explained to the Crakers that the infected people were pieces of "a bad dream that Crake is dreaming."

By evening, they came to the ocean, and Snowman informed the Crakers that they had arrived at their new home.

ANALYSIS

Jimmy's decision to change his name to Snowman signals an important moment of self-transformation, one that the reader has been waiting for since the beginning of the novel. Up until this moment, the narrative has shifted back and forth between Snowman and Jimmy, creating the illusion that the two men are different people. Thus, the moment Jimmy walked into the Paradice bubble and introduced himself to the Children of Crake as Snowman marks both a symbolic point in the character's development as well as a significant moment in the plot. With regard to character development, the adoption of a new name indicates self-determination. "Jimmy" had felt powerless in the face of his father's disappointment and his mother's abandonment, and he always played second fiddle to Crake. While working at Paradice, Crake tried to revive Jimmy's old Extinctathon codename, "Thickney." However, Jimmy never identified with this name, partly because he never excelled at Extinctathon and partly because he didn't choose the name himself. When Jimmy takes the name Snowman, it is a self-directed act of transformation. His new name allows him to adopt a new persona, one perhaps better suited for life in a devastated world.

The Crakers' exit from Paradice at once echoes and reverses the meaning of the biblical story of Paradise lost. In the Bible, God expels Adam and Eve from the Garden of Eden for disobeying his order not to eat from the Tree of Knowledge. For this reason, their departure from Paradise is bound up with notions of exile and sin. In the case of the Children of Crake, however, their departure from Paradice does not represent a form of exile or punishment. In fact, Oryx had taught them about plants and animals specifically to prepare them for life in the outside world. Furthermore, the Crakers' departure was not linked to any sin on their part, but rather to the sin of their father and creator, Crake, the God-like man who made Paradice and placed them there in the first place. Unlike Adam and Eve, who had grown self-conscious of their bodies upon their ejection from the Garden and tried to cover themselves with foliage, the Crakers remained perfectly unaware of their nakedness as they forged into their new world. In other words, they left Paradice with their innocence fully intact.

To add to the religious imagery implied by the name "Paradice," Jimmy, now renamed Snowman, takes on the symbolic role of a prophet shepherding his people across the desert to the promised land—that is, through No Man's Land and toward their new home by the ocean. Snowman also plays the role of prophet in the sense that he teaches his flock of followers what they need to know to survive. Already in his first meeting with the Crakers, Snowman began to spin fictions that attempted to help the naïve and sheltered tribe make sense of a complex, chaotic, and confusing world. The stories he invented formed the beginnings of a new mythology that, as the reader learned way back in Chapter 5, has since become increasingly complicated and detailed. Snowman is admittedly an improbable shepherd, and though he's quite cavalier about telling the Crakers' made-up tales, he has nonetheless taken his responsibility for them seriously.

CHAPTERS 14 & 15

SUMMARY

In the present time, Snowman packs as many supplies as he can carry and leaves Paradice. He makes his way out of the Compound and begins to cross No Man's Land, on his way back to the Crakers. As the noon heat approaches he climbs a tree and shields himself in its shade. His foot throbs, and he considers what would happen if he died up in the tree. After a couple hours of rest, he climbs down and continues on his way.

Snowman arrives back near where the Crakers live. When he approaches the Craker village, he hears an unusual noise that sounds like men and women chanting "Amen." As he gets closer, Snowman observes a statue with a head and a body made of ragged cloths. The Crakers notice Snowman and welcome him back. They tell him they've been calling him, and Snowman realizes they were chanting his name, not "Amen." He also realizes that the Crakers have created a statue of his likeness, an idol meant to carry their voices to him. Snowman recalls Crake's warning: "As soon as they start doing art, we're in trouble."

The Crakers ask if Snowman's journey into the sky was difficult. They believe that Crake lives in the sky, and they assumed the tornado had taken Snowman there. Snowman explains that the tornado brought Crake down to earth and that they visited in Paradice, the place they all came from. The Crakers express their desire to go see Crake, but Snowman tells them Crake turned himself into a plant.

One of the women notices Snowman's swollen foot, and a group converges around him to purr over his injury. The pain diminishes, but the swelling doesn't fully abate. The Crakers bring fish for Snowman to eat, and he watches as children dismantle the idol, imagining that it's his real body they're tearing apart.

Abraham Lincoln informs Snowman that a group of three others like him came, one woman and two men. Others explain that the men looked angry and that one of them carried a "noisy stick"—a gun. The group retreated further along the beach when the Crakers tried to approach them. Snowman's mind races, thinking about the other survivors and imagining the worst.

The next day Snowman wakes before dawn, climbs down from his tree, hobbles to the shore, and washes his wounded foot in the water. His wound is worse than ever, and he realizes the antibiotic cocktail he'd injected himself with in Paradice has worn off. He removes his sheet and, wearing nothing but his baseball cap, proceeds along the beach. He follows a trail of human footprints toward a column of smoke rising in the distance.

Through a veil of leaves, he looks at a group of three people sitting around a fire and roasting some animal. The group looks battered and thin, and one of the men has a spraygun. Snowman wonders whether to approach them as a friend or a foe. He whispers to himself, "What do you want me to do?" The voice of Oryx speaks in his mind: "Oh, Jimmy, you were so funny." Next comes Crake's voice: "Don't let me down." Snowman thinks to himself: "Time to go."

ANALYSIS

At the end of a novel that has staged a symbolic battle between the sciences and the arts, the Crakers' statue of Snowman suggests that art may have won out, if only just barely. On the one hand, it's important to recognize the fact that the Crakers are flourishing in the postapocalyptic world and that this in itself is a sign of Crake's scientific achievement. Yet the Crakers are also developing into a tribe of quasi-religious people, which contravenes Crake's desire for them to live without any metaphysics or faith. And as they begin to construct religious idols in their attempt to influence the world around them, the Crakers violate their creator's original designs even further. In addition to the Crakers' experiments with statue building, Snowman's survival also indicates that the final victory might go to art. Crake may have succeeded in destroying human civilization and ensuring the survival of his own creations, but when he died, he left everything in Snowman's hands, and it is his influence that will dictate the Crakers' destiny from now on. And given the Crakers' construction of a Snowman idol, it is likely that Snowman will become an important part of their pantheon, alongside Oryx and Crake.

The budding leadership sensibility of the Craker named Abraham Lincoln also threatens to undermine Crake's designs. In this chapter Abraham Lincoln is the first to inform Snowman of the group of human survivors, and he appears to take more responsibility for the Crakers than anyone other than Snowman. Snowman noted Abraham Lincoln's leadership qualities back in Chapter 7. At that time, he also reflected on Crake's warning that leaders inevitably turn into tyrants. Crake's theory about leaders likely stemmed from his recognition of the tyranny of corporations. Crake knew well the power that corporations held. In fact, he wielded the power of

RejoovenEsense against itself when he used that corporation's vast resources to develop BlyssPluss and the Crakers. Crake's dislike of corporate tyranny gave birth to his desire for the Crakers to live in a nonhierarchical society with no authority figures. However, Abraham Lincoln's growing tendency to take charge suggests that the Crakers could eventually evolve into a more hierarchical society. And when considered alongside their nascent religiosity and art-making abilities, the Crakers may eventually develop into the same kind of complex society that Crake just destroyed.

The novel's ambiguous ending emphasizes the uncertainty of the future. With his foot infection having advanced past recovery, Snowman will likely suffer a painful death in the near future. In the present moment, though, he remains unsure about how to approach the group of survivors. He doesn't know whether the strangers are friends or enemies, and the novel leaves the reader unsure what Snowman has chosen to do next. When Snowman tells himself, "time to go," it isn't clear whether that means it's time to approach the group or time to walk away from it. Evidence could support either reading. Snowman has been so lonely throughout the book, and his only moments of joy have come from entertaining the possibility of other survivors. From this perspective, it seems likely that he has chosen to approach the group. On the other hand, Snowman has learned to manage his loneliness by retreating into memory, and by now, he might prefer the companionship of the voices in his head. In the novel's final moments, Snowman hears the voices of Oryx and Crake, suggesting that they are with him in spirit. Snowman's imagined trio therefore symbolically mirrors the group of survivors around the fire. Which group will he choose?

IMPORTANT QUOTATIONS EXPLAINED

1. Strange to think of the endless labour, the digging, the hammering, the carving, the lifting, the drilling, day by day, year by year, century by century; and now the endless crumbling that must be going on everywhere. Sandcastles in the wind.

This quotation appears in Chapter 3 as Snowman looks at the ruins of his fallen civilization and contemplates how even those things that appear most solid turn out to be fragile. After the daily afternoon storm, Snowman makes his way to a collapsed bridge where he can shower in the runoff and fill his empty beer bottles with drinking water. As he approaches the broken bridge, Snowman notices a sign reading "Men at Work," which prompts him to consider the extraordinary amount of human labor that went into the design and construction of such a feat of engineering. Yet for all that labor, and in spite of its apparent solidity, it didn't take much for the cement bridge to buckle and collapse into ruin. For Snowman, the bridge symbolizes civilization as a whole, a vast and interconnected human invention that took centuries to build and just one generation to destroy. Although Snowman mourns the destruction of civilization, his observation also has a spiritual quality. Just as the construction is "endless," Snowman suggests that the crumbling is similarly "endless." The double use of "endless" suggests an eternal, cosmic cycle of life and death, creation and destruction.

2. When did the body first set out on its own adventures? Snowman thinks; after having ditched its old travelling companions, the mind and the soul, for whom it had once been considered a mere corrupt vessel or else a puppet acting out their dramas for them, or else bad company, leading the other two astray.

Snowman has this thought in Chapter 4, in the midst of recollections about how he and Crake used to watch graphic videos of violence and sex on the internet. Adopting an unusually philosophical tone, Snowman asks himself a rhetorical question about desire. He wants to know when and why a person leaves behind their various intellectual and moral hang-ups (i.e., "the mind and the soul") and allows themselves to pursue whatever the body desires. Snowman suggests that the body is typically considered a mere puppet taking its commands from some higher entity. Yet Snowman believes that something different was happening when he and Crake started consuming such graphic media. Instead of taking orders from "the mind" or "the soul," Snowman claims that his body abandoned these "old travelling companions" and "set out on its own adventures" instead. The fact that Snowman interjects this thought into the midst of his own recollections suggests that he still feels shame about his early interest in watching executions and pornography. As such, he tries to justify his own desires to himself.

3.   Nature is to zoos as God is to churches.

Crake speaks these words to Jimmy in Chapter 8 during a discussion about the moral implications of creating genetically modified animals like wolvogs. Students at Watson-Crick developed the wolvog, a hybrid dog–wolf creature whose friendly appearance conceals a dangerous ferocity. Jimmy worried that the creation of such animals crosses an ethical line. But Crake dismissed Jimmy's concern as naïve, and he rejected the implicit distinction Jimmy made between the natural and the unnatural. Crake articulated his critique of Jimmy's thinking in the cryptic analogy: "Nature is to zoos as God is to churches." Crake, who was an atheist, believed that God is a human invention. He also believed that churches are institutions that exist to make the abstract idea of God seem concrete and real and thereby imprison people in false notions, such as the distinction between good and evil. Crake suggested a similar logic at work in "Nature" with a capital N. Similar to God, Nature is an abstract idea made to seem real through institutions like zoos. Just as a zoo imprisons animals, the concept of Nature is an ideological cage that imprisons people like Jimmy in a false distinction between the natural and the unnatural.

4. He knew he was faltering, trying to keep his footing.
    Everything in his life was temporary, ungrounded.
    Language itself had lost its solidity; it had become thin,
    contingent, slippery, a viscid film on which he was sliding
    around like an eyeball on a plate.

This quotation appears at the end of Chapter 10, soon after Jimmy learned about his mother's execution. In the wake of this devastating news, Jimmy spiraled into a deep depression. He retreated from his already limited social life, and he began to drink alone at night, attempting to drown his sorrows. Jimmy lost his sense of purpose, and he also began to lose his footing in reality. The growing sensation that everything in Jimmy's life was "temporary" echoes a similar quotation from Chapter 3, in which Snowman reflects on just how temporary civilization turned out to be. More important, however, is Jimmy's feeling that language "had lost its solidity." As a self-defined "words guy" who had devoted years to studying rhetoric, Jimmy felt most grounded in language, which had the extraordinary power to produce meaning in an otherwise meaningless world. Without this power to create meaning, the world devolved into a disorienting chaos. Although Jimmy later emerged from his depression when Crake offered him a job at RejoovenEsense, the sense of disorientation and meaninglessness indicated in this quotation will return to afflict Snowman in the aftermath of the apocalypse.

5.   "Immortality," said Crake, "is a concept. If you take
        'mortality' as being, not death, but the foreknowledge of it
        and the fear of it, then 'immortality' is the absence of such
        fear. Babies are immortal. Edit out the fear and you'll be . . ."
        "Sounds like Applied Rhetoric 101," said Jimmy.
        "What?"
        "Never mind. Martha Graham stuff."

This conversation takes place in Chapter 12, when Crake first revealed to Jimmy the experiments he'd been conducting on the human genome. Crake explained his hope that his new breed of humans would not have a concept of mortality and hence wouldn't fear death. This would enable them to possess a feeling of immortality without actually living forever. When Jimmy interrupted, saying that his explanation sounded like it came directly from an elementary course in Applied Rhetoric, Crake didn't understand what he meant. Jimmy didn't pursue the matter, dismissing his interjection as "Martha Graham stuff"—that is, it had something to do with the kind of thinking that takes place in the humanities rather than the sciences. Though Jimmy didn't push his point, his interjection nonetheless demonstrates an important irony in Crake's perspective and in scientific thinking more generally. Crake prided himself on his logical thinking, and this pride frequently led him to dismiss Jimmy's more philosophical perspective. Yet beneath Crake's commitment to rationality lay a deeper foundation in philosophy that quietly guided his scientific inquiries. Jimmy drew attention to this underlying condition when he pointed out that Crake's ideas about immortality—which in turn motivated his experiments—were essentially philosophical.

KEY FACTS

FULL TITLE
Oryx and Crake

AUTHOR
Margaret Atwood

TYPE OF WORK
Novel

GENRE
Speculative fiction; dystopian fiction; postapocalyptic fiction

LANGUAGE
English

TIME AND PLACE WRITTEN
Canada, late 1990s and early 2000s

DATE OF FIRST PUBLICATION
May 2003

PUBLISHER
McClelland and Stewart (Canada); Bloomsbury (UK);
Doubleday (US)

NARRATOR
The narrator is anonymous. The narrator mostly speaks with
an objective perspective but occasionally mimics Snowman's
thoughts, which makes the narrator's voice sound more like
Snowman's.

POINT OF VIEW
Snowman's point of view dominates *Oryx and Crake*, but
instead of Snowman speaking for himself, the narrator speaks
about Snowman in the third person. The narrator has full
access to Snowman's thoughts and feelings and so describes
everything in the world as Snowman sees it from his subjective
perspective.

TONE

Cynical and mournful. Snowman's narrative recounts the rise of Crake's scientific ambitions, which resulted in the fall of human civilization.

TENSE

The chapters following Snowman are narrated in the present tense, and the chapters following Snowman's past self, Jimmy, are narrated in the past tense.

SETTING (TIME)

Near the end of the twenty-first century

SETTING (PLACE)

The East Coast of the United States, somewhere in the mid-Atlantic

PROTAGONIST

Snowman (aka Jimmy)

MAJOR CONFLICT

The major conflict plays out between Crake and Snowman and the ideals each man stands for: whereas Crake stands for scientific progress and rational solutions to the world's problems, Snowman stands for a more complex and humanistic view that seeks to understand rather than solve the world's problems.

RISING ACTION

On his way to Paradice, Snowman remembers how he came to work at the facility when Crake was in the final stages of developing his two-part plan, which included the BlyssPluss pill and a tribe of genetically enhanced humans. Both men fell in love with Oryx and had relationships with her.

CLIMAX

Once he arrives at Paradice, Snowman remembers when he first realized that Crake's BlyssPluss pill caused the global outbreak of a deadly plague and that Oryx had unknowingly helped prepare the way for Crake's plan.

FALLING ACTION

Snowman remembers how, in the first hours of the outbreak, Crake returned to Paradice with Oryx and slit her throat, prompting Snowman to shoot Crake.

KEY FACTS

THEMES

The danger of scientific advancement; the dominance of corporate power; the devaluation of art

MOTIFS

Voices; memory; playing God

SYMBOLS

Blood and Roses; Alex the Parrot; the children of Oryx

FORESHADOWING

Foreshadowing permeates most the narrative, which involves Snowman remembering the events that led to the postapocalyptic conditions of his present situation. Each event brings the reader closer to an ultimate understanding of the event that wiped out most of the world's population and Snowman's personal role in it. For example, Snowman recalls Crake's hypothesis about HelthWyzer using vitamin pills to distribute newly developed diseases, which in hindsight he now recognizes as a forerunner to the plague Crake spread via his BlyssPluss pills.

Study Questions

1. *Why did Jimmy rename himself Snowman, and what is the significance of his new name?*

Jimmy renamed himself Snowman because he felt the need to adopt a new persona for the new world in which he lived. Crake's plague decimated the majority of the planet, including the only two people who still meant something to Jimmy. When Oryx and Crake died, a part of Jimmy died as well. Thus, just before Jimmy introduced himself to the Children of Crake, he adopted his new name. Now radically transformed, Snowman led the Crakers out of Paradise and into a world that was itself radically transformed. Thus, his new name prepared him symbolically and psychologically for his new life in a postapocalyptic world.

But why did he change his name to Snowman, and what does that particular name mean? As the narrator explains in Chapter 1, Snowman is short for Abominable Snowman, which refers to the ape-like Yeti creature said to live in the Himalayas. Symbolically, Snowman's new name both links him to and differentiates him from Crake and Oryx. It links his to his friends, since both of them were known by adopted names. Crake's original name was Glenn, but Snowman never found out Oryx's original name. Yet Snowman's name also differentiates him from Crake and Oryx, since his friends chose names of extinct species that really used to exist. By contrast, Snowman named himself after a mythical creature, at once "existing and not existing, flickering at the edges of blizzards." On the one hand, Snowman's new name represents an intentional offense against Crake, who made a rule that no one at Paradice could choose a name "for which a physical equivalent . . . could not be demonstrated." On the other hand, Snowman's new name reflects his current existential status, in which he feels like he's flickering between past and present, possibly the last member of an endangered species on the brink of extinction.

2. *Does Snowman hate his mother?*

At several points in the novel Snowman reflects on how much he hates his mother, who abandoned him when he was a young boy and added insult to injury by taking his beloved pet rakunk with her. Snowman certainly felt angry about her departure, and he harbored deep feelings of resentment toward her throughout his youth. However, when considered carefully, it is clear that Snowman has a much more complex attitude toward his mother than simple hatred. When he was very young, Snowman loved his mother intensely, but the intensity of his love also caused confusion. Confusion arose particularly when his mother fell into a deepening depression that prevented her from giving Snowman the attention he craved. Snowman desperately wanted to cheer her up, and he tried to counter her mood swings with amusing antics but to no avail. At times Snowman's desire to cure his mother's depression left him wondering whether the sadness belonged to him or to her.

All these confusing emotions became further mixed up and intensified when Snowman's mother chose to run away. Outwardly Snowman pretended that his mother's departure didn't bother him. He told Crake as much and stopped going to therapy almost as soon as he started. Inwardly, however, he felt torn up, and a sense of hatred grew. Over the course of his youth, Snowman continued to feel resentment toward his mother, especially since he had to undergo frequent CorpSeCorps interrogations about her participation in activist organizations. Yet for all the negative feelings he had for his mother, Snowman also never stopped mourning her absence, which becomes clear in Chapter 10, when CorpSeCorps agents show him a video of his mother's execution. The news of his mother's death devastated him, and in the weeks following the Corpsmen's visit, he spiraled into depression. The profound sadness Snowman experienced upon learning of her death suggests that, far from simply hating his mother, Snowman retained a complicated love for her.

3. *What is the significance of the name "Paradice?"*

Paradice is the secret facility where Crake developed his genetically modified breed of humans, and the name references the biblical Paradise, also known as the Garden of Eden. According to the biblical account, God placed Adam and Eve, the first man and woman, in the Garden of Eden, where they would have everything they needed to live in perfect harmony and comfort. The only restriction God placed on Adam and Eve was that they could not eat the fruit from the Tree of Knowledge. But Adam and Eve defied the taboo, and God cast them out of Eden, leaving them to wander alone in exile. In the Christian tradition, the fall of Adam and Eve from God's grace and their subsequent loss of Paradise represents the "fallen" condition of humankind, which must attempt to regain Paradise by purging itself of sin.

Crake's Paradice echoes the biblical Paradise in the sense that it's the place where the first members of a new human race live in perfect harmony with each other and their environment, just like Adam and Eve. The choice of the name Paradice also casts Crake as God, which is ironic given Crake's resolute atheism. However, this sense of irony gives the name Paradice an additional twist of meaning that revises biblical tradition. Whereas the Bible frames Adam and Eve's departure from the Garden as a banishment into exile, Crake actually meant for his new humans to leave Paradice. Furthermore, instead of seeking redemption for their own souls, as the Christian tradition calls for, Crake intended for his new humans to be the agents of redemption. That is, he wanted them to go out and redeem the world stained by human civilization. The full significance of the name Paradice therefore stems from the way it both echoes and revises biblical tradition.

STUDY QUESTIONS

How to Write Literary Analysis

The Literary Essay: A Step-by-Step Guide

When you read for pleasure, your only goal is enjoyment. You might find yourself reading to get caught up in an exciting story, to learn about an interesting time or place, or just to pass time. Maybe you're looking for inspiration, guidance, or a reflection of your own life. There are as many different, valid ways of reading a book as there are books in the world.

When you read a work of literature in an English class, however, you're being asked to read in a special way: you're being asked to perform *literary analysis*. To analyze something means to break it down into smaller parts and then examine how those parts work, both individually and together. Literary analysis involves examining all the parts of a novel, play, short story, or poem—elements such as character, setting, tone, and imagery—and thinking about how the author uses those elements to create certain effects.

A literary essay isn't a book review: you're not being asked whether or not you liked a book or whether you'd recommend it to another reader. A literary essay also isn't like the kind of book report you wrote when you were younger, when your teacher wanted you to summarize the book's action. A high school or college–level literary essay asks, "How does this piece of literature actually work?" "How does it do what it does?" and, "Why might the author have made the choices he or she did?"

The Seven Steps

No one is born knowing how to analyze literature; it's a skill and a process you can master. As you gain more practice with this kind of thinking and writing, you'll be able to craft a method that works best for you. But until then, here are seven basic steps to writing a well-constructed literary essay:

1. *Ask questions*
2. *Collect evidence*
3. *Construct a thesis*

4. Develop and organize arguments
5. Write the introduction
6. Write the body paragraphs
7. Write the conclusion

1. Ask Questions

When you're assigned a literary essay in class, your teacher will often provide you with a list of writing prompts. Lucky you! Now all you have to do is choose one. Do yourself a favor and pick a topic that interests you. You'll have a much better (not to mention easier) time if you start off with something you enjoy thinking about. If you are asked to come up with a topic by yourself, though, you might start to feel a little panicked. Maybe you have too many ideas—or none at all. Don't worry. Take a deep breath and start by asking yourself these questions:

- **What struck you?** Did a particular image, line, or scene linger in your mind for a long time? If it fascinated you, chances are you can draw on it to write a fascinating essay.

- **What confused you?** Maybe you were surprised to see a character act in a certain way, or maybe you didn't understand why the book ended the way it did. Confusing moments in a work of literature are like a loose thread in a sweater: if you pull on it, you can unravel the entire thing. Ask yourself why the author chose to write about that character or scene the way he or she did, and you might tap into some important insights about the work as a whole.

- **Did you notice any patterns?** Is there a phrase that the main character uses constantly or an image that repeats throughout the book? If you can figure out how that pattern weaves through the work and what the significance of that pattern is, you've almost got your entire essay mapped out.

- **Did you notice any contradictions or ironies?** Great works of literature are complex; great literary essays recognize and explain those complexities. Maybe the title of the work seems to contradict its content (for example, the play *Happy Days* shows its two characters buried up to their waists in dirt). Maybe the main character acts one way around his or her family and a completely different way around his or her friends and associates. If you can find a way to explain a work's contradictory elements, you've got the seeds of a great essay.

At this point, you don't need to know exactly what you're going to say about your topic; you just need a place to begin your exploration. You can help direct your reading and brainstorming by formulating your topic as a *question*, which you'll then try to answer in your essay. The best questions invite critical debates and discussions, not just a rehashing of the summary. Remember, you're looking for something you can *prove or argue* based on evidence you find in the text. Finally, remember to keep the scope of your question in mind: is this a topic you can adequately address within the word or page limit you've been given? Conversely, is this a topic big enough to fill the required length?

GOOD QUESTIONS

"Are Romeo and Juliet's parents responsible for the deaths of their children?"

"Why do pigs keep showing up in Lord of the Flies*?"*

"Are Dr. Frankenstein and his monster alike? How?"

BAD QUESTIONS

"What happens to Scout in To Kill a Mockingbird*?"*

"What do the other characters in Julius Caesar *think about Caesar?"*

"How does Hester Prynne in The Scarlet Letter *remind me of my sister?"*

---

2. COLLECT EVIDENCE

Once you know what question you want to answer, it's time to scour the book for things that will help you answer the question. Don't worry if you don't know what you want to say yet—right now you're just collecting ideas and material and letting it all percolate. Keep track of passages, symbols, images, or scenes that deal with your topic. Eventually, you'll start making connections between these examples, and your thesis will emerge.

Here's a brief summary of the various parts that compose each and every work of literature. These are the elements that you will analyze in your essay and that you will offer as evidence to support your arguments. For more on the parts of literary works, see the Glossary of Literary Terms at the end of this section.

ELEMENTS OF STORY These are the *what*s of the work—what happens, where it happens, and to whom it happens.

- **Plot:** All the events and actions of the work.

- **Character:** The people who act and are acted on in a literary work. The main character of a work is known as the *protagonist*.

- **Conflict:** The central tension in the work. In most cases, the protagonist wants something, while opposing forces (antagonists) hinder the protagonist's progress.

- **Setting:** When and where the work takes place. Elements of setting include location, time period, time of day, weather, social atmosphere, and economic conditions.

- **Narrator:** The person telling the story. The narrator may straightforwardly report what happens, convey the subjective opinions and perceptions of one or more characters, or provide commentary and opinion in his or her own voice.

- **Themes:** The main idea or message of the work—usually an abstract idea about people, society, or life in general. A work may have many themes, which may be in tension with one another.

ELEMENTS OF STYLE These are the *how*s—how the characters speak, how the story is constructed, and how language is used throughout the work.

- **Structure and organization:** How the parts of the work are assembled. Some novels are narrated in a linear, chronological fashion, while others skip around in time. Some plays follow a traditional three- or five-act structure, while others are a series of loosely connected scenes. Some authors deliberately leave gaps in their work, leaving readers to puzzle out the missing information. A work's structure and organization can tell you a lot about the kind of message it wants to convey.

- **Point of view:** The perspective from which a story is told. In *first-person point of view*, the narrator involves himself or herself in the story. ("I went to the store"; "We watched in horror as the bird slammed into the window.") A first-person narrator is usually the protagonist of the work, but not always. In *third-person point of view*, the narrator does not participate in the story. A third-person narrator may closely follow a specific character, recounting that individual character's thoughts or experiences, or it may be what we call an *omniscient* narrator. Omniscient narrators see and know all: they can witness any event in any time or place and are privy to the inner thoughts and feelings of all characters. Remember that the narrator and the author are not the same thing!

- **Diction:** Word choice. Whether a character uses dry, clinical language or flowery prose with lots of exclamation points can tell you a lot about his or her attitude and personality.

- **Syntax:** Word order and sentence construction. Syntax is a crucial part of establishing an author's narrative voice. Ernest Hemingway, for example, is known for writing in very short, straightforward sentences, while James Joyce characteristically wrote in long, extremely complicated lines.

- **Tone:** The mood or feeling of the text. Diction and syntax often contribute to the tone of a work. A novel written in short, clipped sentences that use small, simple words might feel brusque, cold, or matter-of-fact.

- **Imagery:** Language that appeals to the senses, representing things that can be seen, smelled, heard, tasted, or touched.

- **Figurative language:** Language that is not meant to be interpreted literally. The most common types of figurative language are *metaphors* and *similes*, which compare two unlike things in order to suggest a similarity between them— for example, "All the world's a stage," or "The moon is like a ball of green cheese." (Metaphors say one thing *is* another thing; similes claim that one thing is *like* another thing.)

---

3. CONSTRUCT A THESIS

When you've examined all the evidence you've collected and know how you want to answer the question, it's time to write your thesis statement. A *thesis* is a claim about a work of literature that needs to be supported by evidence and arguments. The thesis statement is the heart of the literary essay, and the bulk of your paper will be spent trying to prove this claim. A good thesis will be:

- **Arguable.** "*The Great Gatsby* describes New York society in the 1920s" isn't a thesis—it's a fact.

- **Provable through textual evidence.** "*Hamlet* is a confusing but ultimately very well-written play" is a weak thesis because it offers the writer's personal opinion about the book. Yes, it's arguable, but it's not a claim that can be proved or supported with examples taken from the play itself.

- **Surprising.** "Both George and Lenny change a great deal in *Of Mice and Men*" is a weak thesis because it's obvious. A really strong thesis will argue for a reading of the text that is not immediately apparent.

- **Specific.** "Dr. Frankenstein's monster tells us a lot about the human condition" is *almost* a really great thesis statement, but it's still too vague. What does the writer mean by "a lot"? *How* does the monster tell us so much about the human condition?

GOOD THESIS STATEMENTS

Question: In *Romeo and Juliet*, which is more powerful in shaping the lovers' story: fate or foolishness?

Thesis: "Though Shakespeare defines Romeo and Juliet as 'star-crossed lovers,' and images of stars and planets appear throughout the play, a closer examination of that celestial imagery reveals that the stars are merely witnesses to the characters' foolish activities and not the causes themselves."

Question: How does the bell jar function as a symbol in Sylvia Plath's *The Bell Jar*?

Thesis: "A bell jar is a bell-shaped glass that has three basic uses: to hold a specimen for observation, to contain gases, and to maintain a vacuum. The bell jar appears in each of these capacities in *The Bell Jar*, Plath's semi-autobiographical novel, and each appearance marks a different stage in Esther's mental breakdown."

Question: Would Piggy in *The Lord of the Flies* make a good island leader if he were given the chance?

Thesis: "Though the intelligent, rational, and innovative Piggy has the mental characteristics of a good leader, he ultimately lacks the social skills necessary to be an effective one. Golding emphasizes this point by giving Piggy a foil in the charismatic Jack, whose magnetic personality allows him to capture and wield power effectively, if not always wisely."

LITERARY ANALYSIS

4. Develop and Organize Arguments

The reasons and examples that support your thesis will form the middle paragraphs of your essay. Since you can't really write your thesis statement until you know how you'll structure your argument, you'll probably end up working on steps 3 and 4 at the same time. There's no single method of argumentation that will work in every context. One essay prompt might ask you to compare and contrast two characters, while another asks you to trace an image through a given work of literature. These questions require different kinds of answers and therefore different kinds of arguments. Below, we'll discuss three common kinds of essay prompts and some strategies for constructing a solid, well-argued case.

Types of Literary Essays

- **Compare and contrast**

    Compare and contrast the characters of Huck and Jim in The Adventures of Huckleberry Finn.

    Chances are you've written this kind of essay before. In an academic literary context, you'll organize your arguments the same way you would in any other class. You can either go *subject by subject* or *point by point*. In the former, you'll discuss one character first and then the second. In the latter, you'll choose several traits (attitude toward life, social status, images and metaphors associated with the character) and devote a paragraph to each. You may want to use a mix of these two approaches—for example, you may want to spend a paragraph apiece broadly sketching Huck's and Jim's personalities before transitioning to a paragraph or two describing a few key points of comparison. This can be a highly effective strategy if you want to make a counterintuitive argument—that, despite seeming to be totally different, the two characters or objects being compared are actually similar in a very important way (or vice versa). Remember that your essay should reveal something fresh or unexpected about the text, so think beyond the obvious parallels and differences.

- **Trace**

  Choose an image—for example, birds, knives, or eyes—and trace that image throughout Macbeth.

  Sounds pretty easy, right? All you need to do is read the play, underline every appearance of a knife in *Macbeth* and then list them in your essay in the order they appear, right? Well, not exactly. Your teacher doesn't want a simple catalog of examples. He or she wants to see you make *connections* between those examples—that's the difference between summarizing and analyzing. In the *Macbeth* example, think about the different contexts in which knives appear in the play and to what effect. In *Macbeth*, there are real knives and imagined knives; knives that kill and knives that simply threaten. Categorize and classify your examples to give them some order. Finally, always keep the overall effect in mind. After you choose and analyze your examples, you should come to some greater understanding about the work, as well as the role of your chosen image, symbol, or phrase in developing the major themes and stylistic strategies of that work.

- **Debate**

  Is the society depicted in 1984 *good for its citizens?*

  In this kind of essay, you're being asked to debate a moral, ethical, or aesthetic issue regarding the work. You might be asked to judge a character or group of characters *(Is Caesar responsible for his own demise?)* or the work itself (*Is* Jane Eyre *a feminist novel?*). For this kind of essay, there are two important points to keep in mind. First, don't simply base your arguments on your personal feelings and reactions. Every literary essay expects you to read and analyze the work, so search for evidence in the text. What do characters in *1984* have to say about the government of Oceania? What images does Orwell use that might give you a hint about his attitude toward the government? As in any debate, you also need to make sure that you define all the necessary terms before you begin to argue your case. What does it mean to be a "good" society? What makes a novel "feminist"? You should define your terms right up front, in the first paragraph after your introduction.

Second, remember that strong literary essays make contrary and surprising arguments. Try to think outside the box. In the *1984* example above, it seems like the obvious answer would be no, the totalitarian society depicted in Orwell's novel is *not* good for its citizens. But can you think of any arguments for the opposite side? Even if your final assertion is that the novel depicts a cruel, repressive, and therefore harmful society, acknowledging and responding to the counterargument will strengthen your overall case.

---

5. WRITE THE INTRODUCTION

Your introduction sets up the entire essay. It's where you present your topic and articulate the particular issues and questions you'll be addressing. It's also where you, as the writer, introduce yourself to your readers. A persuasive literary essay immediately establishes its writer as a knowledgeable, authoritative figure.

An introduction can vary in length depending on the overall length of the essay, but in a traditional five-paragraph essay it should be no longer than one paragraph. However long it is, your introduction needs to:

- **Provide any necessary context.** Your introduction should situate the reader and let him or her know what to expect. What book are you discussing? Which characters? What topic will you be addressing?

- **Answer the "So what?" question.** Why is this topic important, and why is your particular position on the topic noteworthy? Ideally, your introduction should pique the reader's interest by suggesting how your argument is surprising or otherwise counterintuitive. Literary essays make unexpected connections and reveal less-than-obvious truths.

- **Present your thesis.** This usually happens at or very near the end of your introduction.

- **Indicate the shape of the essay to come.** Your reader should finish reading your introduction with a good sense of the scope of your essay as well as the path you'll take toward proving your thesis. You don't need to spell out every step, but you do need to suggest the organizational pattern you'll be using.

Your introduction should not:

- **Be vague.** Beware of the two killer words in literary analysis: *interesting* and *important*. Of course, the work, question, or example is interesting and important—that's why you're writing about it!

- **Open with any grandiose assertions.** Many student readers think that beginning their essays with a flamboyant statement, such as "Since the dawn of time, writers have been fascinated by the topic of free will," makes them sound important and commanding. In fact, it sounds pretty amateurish.

- **Wildly praise the work.** Another typical mistake student writers make is extolling the work or author. Your teacher doesn't need to be told that "Shakespeare is perhaps the greatest writer in the English language." You can mention a work's reputation in passing—by referring to *The Adventures of Huckleberry Finn* as "Mark Twain's enduring classic," for example—but don't make a point of bringing it up unless that reputation is key to your argument.

- **Go off-topic.** Keep your introduction streamlined and to the point. Don't feel the need to throw in all kinds of bells and whistles in order to impress your reader—just get to the point as quickly as you can, without skimping on any of the required steps.

---

6. WRITE THE BODY PARAGRAPHS

Once you've written your introduction, you'll take the arguments you developed in step 4 and turn them into your body paragraphs. The organization of this middle section of your essay will largely be determined by the argumentative strategy you use, but no matter how you arrange your thoughts, your body paragraphs need to do the following:

- **Begin with a strong topic sentence.** Topic sentences are like signs on a highway: they tell the readers where they are and where they're going. A good topic sentence not only alerts readers to what issue will be discussed in the following paragraphs but also gives them a sense of what argument will be made *about* that issue. "Rumor and gossip play an important role in *The Crucible*" isn't a strong topic sentence because it doesn't tell us very much. "The community's constant gossiping creates an environment that allows false accusations to flourish" is a much stronger topic sentence—

it not only tells us what the paragraph will discuss (gossip) but how the paragraph will discuss the topic (by showing how gossip creates a set of conditions that leads to the play's climactic action).

- **Fully and completely develop a single thought.** Don't skip around in your paragraph or try to stuff in too much material. Body paragraphs are like bricks: each individual one needs to be strong and sturdy or the entire structure will collapse. Make sure you have really proven your point before moving on to the next one.

- **Use transitions effectively.** Good literary essay writers know that each paragraph must be clearly and strongly linked to the material around it. Think of each paragraph as a response to the one that precedes it. Use transition words and phrases such as *however*, *similarly*, *on the contrary*, *therefore*, and *furthermore* to indicate what kind of response you're making.

---

7. WRITE THE CONCLUSION

Just as you used the introduction to ground your readers in the topic before providing your thesis, you'll use the conclusion to quickly summarize the specifics learned thus far and then hint at the broader implications of your topic. A good conclusion will:

- **Do more than simply restate the thesis.** If your thesis argued that *The Catcher in the Rye* can be read as a Christian allegory, don't simply end your essay by saying, "And that is why *The Catcher in the Rye* can be read as a Christian allegory." If you've constructed your arguments well, this kind of statement will just be redundant.

- **Synthesize the arguments rather than summarizing them.** Similarly, don't repeat the details of your body paragraphs in your conclusion. The readers have already read your essay, and chances are it's not so long that they've forgotten all your points by now.

- **Revisit the "So what?" question.** In your introduction, you made a case for why your topic and position are important. You should close your essay with the same sort of gesture. What do your readers know now that they didn't know before? How will that knowledge help them better appreciate or understand the work overall?

- **Move from the specific to the general.** Your essay has most likely treated a very specific element of the work—a single character, a small set of images, or a particular passage. In your conclusion, try to show how this narrow discussion has wider implications for the work overall. If your essay on *To Kill a Mockingbird* focused on the character of Boo Radley, for example, you might want to include a bit in the conclusion about how he fits into the novel's larger message about childhood, innocence, or family life.

- **Stay relevant.** Your conclusion should suggest new directions of thought, but it shouldn't be treated as an opportunity to pad your essay with all the extra, interesting ideas you came up with during your brainstorming sessions but couldn't fit into the essay proper. Don't attempt to stuff in unrelated queries or too many abstract thoughts.

- **Avoid making overblown closing statements.** A conclusion should open up your highly specific, focused discussion, but it should do so without drawing a sweeping lesson about life or human nature. Making such observations may be part of the point of reading, but it's almost always a mistake in essays, where these observations tend to sound overly dramatic or simply silly.

A+ ESSAY CHECKLIST

Congratulations! If you've followed all the steps we've outlined, you should have a solid literary essay to show for all your efforts. What if you've got your sights set on an A+? To write the kind of superlative essay that will be rewarded with a perfect grade, keep the following rubric in mind. These are the qualities that teachers expect to see in a truly A+ essay. How does yours stack up?

- ✓ Demonstrates a thorough understanding of the book
- ✓ Presents an original, compelling argument
- ✓ Thoughtfully analyzes the text's formal elements
- ✓ Uses appropriate and insightful examples
- ✓ Structures ideas in a logical and progressive order
- ✓ Demonstrates a mastery of sentence construction, transitions, grammar, spelling, and word choice

Suggested Essay Topics

1.   How does Snowman's view of "reality" differ from Crake's?

2.   What is the significance of Crake's understanding of immortality?

3.   Why does Snowman spend so much time trying to remember the meanings of words?

4.   How does Oryx's past shape her view of the world, and how does her perspective differ from those of Snowman and Crake?

5.   Why does Snowman feel responsible for the Crakers?

6.   What is the significance of the mythology that Snowman develops for the Crakers?

GLOSSARY OF LITERARY TERMS

ANTAGONIST
> The entity that acts to frustrate the goals of the *protagonist*. The antagonist is usually another *character* but may also be a nonhuman force.

ANTIHERO / ANTIHEROINE
> A *protagonist* who is not admirable or who challenges notions of what should be considered admirable.

CHARACTER
> A person, animal, or any other thing with a personality that appears in a *narrative*.

CLIMAX
> The moment of greatest intensity in a text or the major turning point in the *plot*.

CONFLICT
> The central struggle that moves the *plot* forward. The conflict can be the *protagonist*'s struggle against fate, nature, society, or another person.

FIRST-PERSON POINT OF VIEW
> A literary style in which the *narrator* tells the story from his or her own *point of view* and refers to himself or herself as "I." The narrator may be an active participant in the story or just an observer.

HERO / HEROINE
> The principal *character* in a literary work or *narrative*.

IMAGERY
> Language that brings to mind sense-impressions, representing things that can be seen, smelled, heard, tasted, or touched.

MOTIF
> A recurring idea, structure, contrast, or device that develops or informs the major *themes* of a work of literature.

NARRATIVE
> A story.

LITERARY ANALYSIS

NARRATOR

The person (sometimes a *character*) who tells a story; the *voice* assumed by the writer. The narrator and the author of the work of literature are not the same thing.

PLOT

The arrangement of the events in a story, including the sequence in which they are told, the relative emphasis they are given, and the causal connections between events.

POINT OF VIEW

The *perspective* that a *narrative* takes toward the events it describes.

PROTAGONIST

The main *character* around whom the story revolves.

SETTING

The location of a *narrative* in time and space. Setting creates mood or atmosphere.

SUBPLOT

A secondary *plot* that is of less importance to the overall story but that may serve as a point of contrast or comparison to the main plot.

SYMBOL

An object, *character*, figure, or color that is used to represent an abstract idea or concept.

SYNTAX

The way the words in a piece of writing are put together to form lines, phrases, or clauses; the basic structure of a piece of writing.

THEME

A fundamental and universal idea explored in a literary work.

TONE

The author's attitude toward the subject or *characters* of a story or poem or toward the reader.

VOICE

An author's individual way of using language to reflect his or her own personality and attitudes. An author communicates voice through *tone*, *diction*, and *syntax*.

LITERARY ANALYSIS

A Note on Plagiarism

Plagiarism—presenting someone else's work as your own—rears its ugly head in many forms. Many students know that copying text without citing it is unacceptable. But some don't realize that even if you're not quoting directly, but instead are paraphrasing or summarizing, it is plagiarism unless you cite the source.

Here are the most common forms of plagiarism:

- Using an author's phrases, sentences, or paragraphs without citing the source

- Paraphrasing an author's ideas without citing the source

- Passing off another student's work as your own

How do you steer clear of plagiarism? You should always acknowledge all words and ideas that aren't your own by using quotation marks around verbatim text or citations like footnotes and endnotes to note another writer's ideas. For more information on how to give credit when credit is due, ask your teacher for guidance or visit www.sparknotes.com.

REVIEW & RESOURCES

Quiz

1. What role does Snowman say he plays in relation to the Crakers?

    A. God
    B. Devil
    C. Angel
    D. Shepherd

2. Whose portrait did Crake use as his secret passkey into the Grandmasters-only area of Extinctathon?

    A. His mother
    B. His father
    C. Jimmy
    D. Oryx

3. What animal does Snowman associate with Oryx?

    A. Owl
    B. Antelope
    C. Snake
    D. Crab

4. Why does Snowman sleep in a tree?

    A. Because he wants to keep an eye on the Children of Crake
    B. Because the height keeps him safe from predators
    C. Because he doesn't want the ocean tides to get him wet
    D. Because the tree provides shelter from afternoon storms

5. Why did Snowman's mother run away?

    A. She leaked secrets about her husband's employer and
    left to save her own life
    B. She eloped with a secret lover
    C. She wanted to see what it would be like to live in the
    pleeblands and travel the world
    D. She believed the scientific research she and her
    husband did was morally wrong

6. Where did Snowman and Crake first encounter Oryx?

    A. In a news story about girls locked in garages
    B. At HelthWyzer High School
    C. On a child pornography site
    D. At the RejoovenEsense Compound

7. Why do the Crakers purr over Snowman when he returns
from Paradice?

    A. To help heal his injured foot
    B. To demonstrate affection
    C. To calm him down
    D. To indicate their displeasure with how long he
    was away

8. What happened to Snowman's childhood pet rakunk, Killer?

    A. She ran away
    B. His mother set her free
    C. She was killed by a bobkitten
    D. His father took her back to his lab

9. What kind of extinct animal did Crake name himself after?

    A. A reptile
    B. A fish
    C. A bird
    D. An insect

10. What did Oryx sell to tourists when she worked for Uncle En?

  A. Paper fans
  B. Candies
  C. Newspapers
  D. Flowers

11. What genetically modified food product sparked global economic and social tensions?

  A. ChickieNobs
  B. SoyOBoy Sardines
  C. Sveltana No-Meat Cocktail Sausages
  D. Happicuppa Coffee

12. How did Snowman learn about his mother's death?

  A. He heard about it on the Noodie News
  B. CorpSeCorps agents showed him a video of her execution
  C. Crake informed him
  D. He saw her executed on the Brainfrizz website

13. What was Crake's BlyssPluss pill designed to do?

  A. Improve the user's libido
  B. Prevent the user from having children
  C. Release a plague
  D. All of the above

14. What was the name of the first company Snowman worked for after graduating from Martha Graham?

  A. CryoJeenyus
  B. NooSkins
  C. AnooYoo
  D. RejoovenEsense

15.   How did Oryx learn English?

    A.   She took a community college course
    B.   She received lessons in exchange for sexual favors
    C.   Uncle En taught her so she could communicate
        with tourists
    D.   She picked it up from watching TV

16.   A herd of what type of animal traps Snowman in the
     RejoovenEsense watchtower?

    A.   Pigoons
    B.   Wolvogs
    C.   Rakunks
    D.   Bobkittens

17.   What lesson did Oryx tell Snowman she learned from her
     experience in the child pornography industry?

    A.   Men are kind at heart
    B.   It's best to stay positive
    C.   Everything has a price
    D.   Children are resilient

18.   What causes Snowman's foot to get infected?

    A.   An insect bite
    B.   A piece of glass
    C.   A wound from a pigoon tusk
    D.   A rusty nail

19.   What sign indicates to Snowman that there may be other
     human survivors?

    A.   Distant laughter
    B.   Rising smoke
    C.   A voice on the radio
    D.   Both A and C

20.   How did Crake's father die?

   A.   He committed suicide
   B.   He succumbed to a viral infection
   C.   His employer had him murdered
   D.   He was accidentally hit by a car in rush hour

21.   What was Snowman's Extinctathon username?

   A.   Thickney
   B.   Komodo
   C.   Hippocampus Ramulosus
   D.   Manatee

22.   What is the main aim of God's Gardeners?

   A.   To plan for the coming apocalypse
   B.   To protest all forms of transgenic engineering
   C.   To encourage a return to traditional farming
        practices
   D.   To put a stop to all consumer meat production

23.   Who or what is MaddAddam?

   A.   A mad scientist
   B.   A collective of scientists
   C.   A computer hacker
   D.   An order of religious fanatics

24.   Why did Snowman kill Crake?

   A.   Because Crake killed Oryx
   B.   Because he was jealous of Crake's success
   C.   Because he wanted to inherit responsibility for
        the Paradice Project
   D.   Because Crake started a plague

25. Which of the following *is not* one of the features of Crake's genetically redesigned humans?

    A.   They emit a citrus scent at dusk to repel mosquitoes
    B.   They are adapted to eat grass, leaves, and roots
    C.   They can live forever
    D.   They have luminescent green eyes

Suggestions for Further Reading

Atwood, Margaret. *In Other Worlds: SF and the Human Imagination*. New York: Anchor Books, 2012.

Bouson, J. Brooks, ed. *Critical Insights: Margaret Atwood*. Ipswich, MA: Salem Press, 2013.

Curtis, Claire. *Postapocalyptic Fiction and the Social Contract: "We'll Not Go Home Again."* Lanham, MD: Lexington Books, 2010.

Hicks, Heather J. *The Post-apocalyptic Novel in the Twenty-First Century*. Houndmills, Basingstoke: Palgrave Macmillan, 2016.

Ku nicki, Sławomir. *Margaret Atwood's Dystopian Fiction: Fire Is Being Eaten*. Newcastle-Upon-Tyne, England: Cambridge Scholars Publishing, 2017.

Macpherson, Heidi Slettedahl. *The Cambridge Introduction to Margaret Atwood*. Cambridge: Cambridge University Press, 2010.

Sheckels, Theodore F. *The Political in Margaret Atwood's Fiction: The Writing on the Wall of the Tent*. London: Routledge, 2016.

Tolan, Fiona. *Margaret Atwood: Feminism and Fiction*. New York: Rodopi, 2007.

Waltoned, Karma, ed. *Margaret Atwood's Apocalypses*. Newcastle-Upon-Tyne, England: Cambridge Scholars Publishing, 2015.

Wisker, Gina. *Margaret Atwood: An Introduction to Critical Views of Her Fiction*. Houndmills, Basingstoke: Palgrave Macmillan, 2012.

REVIEW & RESOURCES

NOTES

NOTES

NOTES

NOTES

NOTES

Notes

NOTES

Notes

NOTES

NOTES

NOTES

NOTES

NOTES